Christine Li
Armstrong

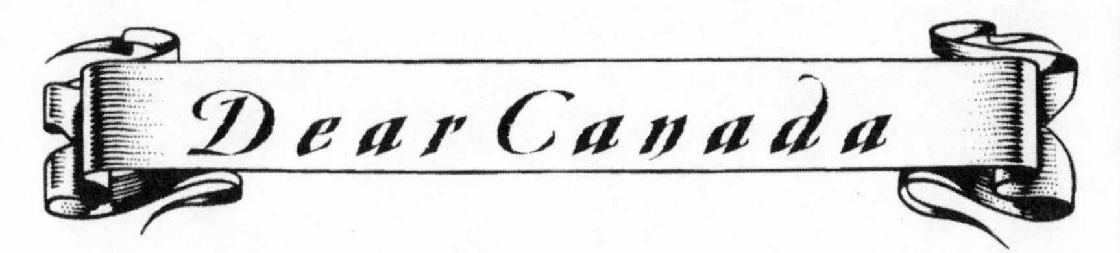

Brothers Far from Home

The World War I Diary of Eliza Bates

BY JEAN LITTLE

Scholastic Canada Ltd.

The Manse
Uxbridge, Ontario
1916

December 25, 1916

It is Christmas Day and I hate my sister Verity. She is a BEAST. She is detestable, mean, cruel and heartless. I know hating her is wicked and I don't care. After all, she despises me. Father and Mother say you should not hate anybody, but I have good reason for thinking my sister is the most abominable girl alive.

Just over an hour ago, she called me "immature" and "a limpet." She talked about me as though I were a changeling. And she did it in front of Jack, True Webb and Rufus West.

How do I know? I heard her. She did not see me there. True had come over from next door carrying her skates and I knew the four of them would all be going out on the pond, so I naturally ran to the hall closet to get my boots. I sat down on the bottom step of the stairs to pull them on. The others were at the far end of the hall by the time I came out and they were so busy arguing that they did not see me. I had one boot almost on when I caught what they were arguing about.

My horrid sister was saying, "Hurry up or the infants will want to tag along."

I thought she meant the Twins, or even Belle, and I began to do up my boot. I knew how she felt. Who would want two eight-year-olds and one nearly-five-year-old tagging along?

Then Jack said, "Eliza's a good scout and she skates pretty well, and she's no infant. We could take *her* along."

And Verity said in a la-di-da voice, "Oh, Jack, she's so immature, always wanting attention. We're used to her but Rufus would find her a dead bore. She'll cling to us like a limpet and giggle and spoil everything. Hurry before she discovers we're gone."

Those were her exact words. They are burned into my soul. They are as bitter as gall.

I don't know what gall is exactly, but I know what the words are as bitter as. Once, when I was the Twins' age, I sneaked a big swallow of vanilla extract right out of the bottle. It smelled so heavenly I could not resist. But the smell was the only good thing about it. I was sure I'd been poisoned and would die before I could spit it all up. Verity's words were that bitter.

True murmured something about it being too bad her sister Cornelia was not well enough to be outdoors yet. She has had the grippe and has been sick in bed ever since we moved here at the end of November.

I have seen her at the window. She stared out at

me as though I was some sort of bug instead of a girl like herself. I smiled at her and waved but she did not wave back. She has a pudding face and does not look like a bosom friend. Having a good friend right next door is what I long for.

Verity latched onto True right away. (True is short for Gertrude. Hardly anyone knows that. I heard her swearing Verity to secrecy. No wonder.) Cornelia is thirteen, just a year older than I, so our being friends would be perfect.

I waited for Jack to stick up for me again, the way Hugo would have. He would have said, "Get your skates, Monkeyshines," and nobody would have argued. I would have answered back, "Hugo, don't call me Monkeyshines," because I always do. But I secretly like it and he knows I do. He understands everything. He never makes me feel like a changeling.

I heard Mother say once, "I'm afraid poor Eliza is the odd man out in our family." She meant to be sympathetic but I felt wounded all the same. Careless words like that can leave bruises on your heart, the kind that don't show but that leave a tender place which goes on hurting for days.

Jack is not Hugo though. He just went along with the rest. They all ran out, shutting the back door ever so softly, and left me sitting on the stairs.

Father came out of his study before I could escape

and said, “Hello there, Diddle Diddle Dumpling.”

It took me a second to figure out why he said this. I had one boot off and one boot on, of course. He meant me to chuckle but I couldn’t do it. I did not even smile. He did not notice my distress. Why would he? He has Hugo and Jack and the War and the church to worry about. I don’t count compared to all of those.

“Annabelle,” he called to Mother, “I just asked a Duck to supper.”

He thinks we don’t know that when he calls people “Ducks” he means “lame ducks.” He invites them to meals all the time. They look so mournful they set my teeth on edge. It is one of the crosses ministers’ families have to bear. Mother says to think how lucky I am to be me instead of one of them, and it will help me be kind. Yet it is hard when you can’t even be spared their company on Christmas Day. Think of the dishes!

With Hugo already at the Front that makes one less at the table. But there are still six of us children plus Mother and Father. Then Grandmother and Aunt Martha are here until New Year’s.

Rufus will be here too, of course. This is Jack’s and his last leave before setting out for England. We’ll see them off on New Year’s Day. I’m trying not to think about it. Hugo’s going was worse, but I hate having my brothers far away.

If Rufus tried to go all the way home to Prince Rupert for Christmas, he would spend almost his whole leave on the train. "Before long, I'll be able to fly home," he said.

He wasn't joking. He and Jack are always talking about the future of flying. (Our Uncle Jack too, which was why he paid for Jack's flying lessons.) Most people think they are crackbrains. After all, who would risk his life in the sky when a perfectly good train would take him where he wants to go.

The way they carry on together, you would think Rufus and Jack had been friends all their lives, not just for the few months they spent at Long Branch while they were training to fly. We will miss Jack when he goes, but we will all miss Rufus too.

After I'd put my boot back in the closet and Father had vanished into the kitchen, I ran up here to the bedroom and cried and cried before I remembered this journal and decided to write it all down and relieve my feelings. Now my eyes are red and puffy and my cheeks feel starched. I will not, will not, *will* not cry any more!!! If I start up again the tears will drip on the page and make the ink run.

Later

I went to the head of the stairs and listened. The skaters are not home yet. The little ones are making a great rumpus playing Mother May I in the downstairs hall with Father. They think it is hilarious when Father turns into "Mother." He hasn't time to play with them like this usually and that makes him better than their Christmas toys. Everyone else is in the kitchen bustling about and gossiping. I heard Aunt Martha telling Mother she didn't look a day over seventy-five. I suppose that is their idea of a joke. If they had spotted me, they would have hailed me down there and had me running my legs off fetching and carrying.

Not one of them is missing me though. I stood in the shadows for ages but I never once heard my name mentioned. I don't fit in and that is all there is to it. And I am *not* going down, Christmas or no Christmas. We opened all the good presents earlier this morning. I saw one handkerchief box with my name on it. It is from Great Aunt Annie. Pinching it did not make my heart beat fast with eager expectation.

Verity will *never* believe I wrote such reams — after she told Grandmother that giving me a journal was a sheer waste of time!

Maybe I should start reading my Christmas book now. I got *A Girl of the Limberlost*. I've already read *Freckles* by the same author and it was wonderful. Freckles was a Limberlost guard with only one hand. The girl in this one is called Elnora. Perhaps she has a hateful sister.

Late Christmas Afternoon

I just read over the *pages* I wrote earlier. I never wrote so much about myself in all my life.

Thinking back, I believe I may have figured out what made Verity so vicious. I believe she's sweet on Rufus. It stands out all over her. She simpers when he comes into a room and she talks about him all the time. These are sure signs. It is ridiculous. She's only seventeen and he is twenty. He probably thinks *she* is immature. If he does, he is absolutely right.

I am loving *A Girl of the Limberlost.* How comforting it is to have a good book waiting for you! Elnora has no sisters to make her life difficult, but her mother is as cold-hearted as the stepmother in Hansel and Gretel.

Fifteen minutes later

Verity gave me the book! I just saw where she wrote in the front, *For Eliza, who likes reading better than anything, with love from her big sister, Verity.* And around the words she drew a wreath of holly berries and leaves and she coloured them with her watercolour paints. They are perfect.

So I suppose I must forgive her even though her spiteful words still make me feel like an orphan lost in the storm.

One thing I am not though is an orphan. How

can you be when your parents have seven children and you come smack in the middle? I should describe them all but it is too big a job for today. Boxing Day will be the perfect time to do it.

I asked True if Cornelia likes to read and she said she doesn't. I will have to find somebody else at school to chum with. Yet the girls I met there were not promising. Maybe it is because Father is a minister. That does make some people nervous. Or it might be my eye.

I was not going to mention my eye problem. It only turns in a little when I am tired or tense. I was very nervous the few weeks I had to go to school before it closed for the Christmas holidays. I tried not to act shy. Maybe I tried too hard. We sit in double desks but there is an uneven number so nobody sat with me.

"You will sit with Cornelia, you lucky thing," Mabel Jackson said with a mean laugh. I wonder what's wrong with Cornelia. Whatever it is, I would rather share a desk with her than with that niminy-piminy Mabel. She reminds me of those porcelain dolls from France, all velvet and lace on the outside but hard as rock underneath. Their curly hair and wide eyes make them seem beautiful, but their faces are proud and pouty when you look again. Mother was given one by her godmother when she was seven. She only takes it out to show people. You cannot play with it. And its prissy little mouth is exactly like Mabel's. She thinks her father being the bank manager makes her a cut above the rest of us. Also she brags about her cousin serving in the battalion that Colonel Sam Sharpe organized back in 1915. I know the 116th was the first Canadian county battalion formed, but the boy is only her second cousin, not her brother.

Mother would be saying "Meow!" at me to warn me not to be so catty. But she does not have to be in the same class as Mabel.

Still Christmas

I fell asleep for an hour and woke up inspired.

This past summer, Verity was given *Jane Eyre* to read. I asked if I would like it and Mother hurried to say it was too old for me. There was something in the way she looked that sent me hotfoot to find where Verity had put it. I started right in and I loved most of it. It is a big book and I lost interest in it once in a while, but parts of it made me cry. I especially liked the bits about her miserable childhood. But I read it all the way to the end. It took me four whole days. (It must have been Mr. Rochester's mad wife locked up in the attic that worried Mother, I suppose.) Anyway, Jane talks to someone she calls "Dear Reader." I've decided to do that too.

You, dear Reader, shall be the friend I long for and I will write this whole journal to you. I'll pretend I'm like Jane Eyre and I'll do my best to make it exciting for you. I am afraid, though, that my life is mostly pretty ordinary. There is no mad person locked in our attic.

Pretending I'm someone in a book will be a thousand times better than writing "Dear Diary" as Verity always does. How do I know, dear Reader? I snooped, of course. It is her own fault for leaving her journal lying about. I think she *wants* me to read it.

You, dear Reader, will keep me company. After Jack and Rufus have gone and I am left with Verity and "the Infants," I won't be so alone if I have you.

Mother is calling me to "lend a hand." I can hear Verity carrying on about how lovely the skating was. You would think Aunt Martha and Verity would have enough hands without mine. I will be back at bedtime probably. I am determined to show them all how mature and faithful I can be. You have helped me already, dear Reader.

Christmas Bedtime

When I got downstairs, True was just leaving. I asked her how Cornelia was.

"Happy as a clam," said True. "She got a new

cross-stitch picture for Christmas and she's stitching away, busy as a bee."

Dear Reader, can you picture a clam or a bee embroidering? I said I'd rather read. And she said their brother Richard was the reader of the family. Before he joined up, he always had his nose in a book.

I asked her what sort of books he read and she waved one hand in the air and said, "Thick, dull ones. History, I think, and philosophy. Nothing I care about, that is certain."

Cornelia sounds less and less kindred. Imagine being strong enough to work on her cross-stitch but too weak to hold up a book. I'll warrant she is also too feeble to "lend a hand" with housework. When I was upstairs, I saw her at the window again, all hunched over something. It must be her embroidery hoop.

At dinner I pulled the wishbone with Charlie and got the long end. What I wished for is that I would meet you in the flesh some day, dear Reader, and I would recognize you at once. You are not supposed to tell wishes, but putting them down in your private journal is not the same as telling.

I am sitting on my side of our double bed, writing. Verity is glancing over at me, unable to believe her eyes. I want to laugh, but I will not so betray myself. She has no idea I wrote in my journal this afternoon while she was swanning about on the pond. After going skating on the Speed River in Guelph all those years before we moved here, a mere pond is a come down.

I confess, dear Reader, that I was furious at my sister *before* she called me immature. It began when we were opening gifts after church. Grandmother had just given us these elegant journals and I had opened my mouth to thank her nicely when Her High Mightyness Verity piped up, "It's no use giving Eliza a journal. She's begun at least five and never written more than a couple of pages in any. She's almost ineligible."

Verity often tries to show off and uses the wrong word. I am what Father calls a voracious reader, but Verity is not. She still has not read *Jane Eyre*. I know because I put it on my own private shelf when I finished it and she has never noticed.

Aunt Martha said, "I assume you mean 'illiterate' or 'illegible,' Verity. But Eliza is extremely literate and her penmanship is quite as readable as yours."

That was nice of her because I don't think she has seen much of my writing. I was supposed to write her a bread-and-butter letter after she sent me two pairs of combinations for my birthday last week. She wrote on the card, "These warm combies are to keep the rectory draughts at bay." (Rectory! — she should know that Presbyterian ministers don't live in rectories but in manses.) The dratted combinations are woolen and they itch like fire. They also sag in the seat. I put down, *Dear Aunt Martha, Mother says to thank you. Sincerely, Eliza Mary Bates.*

I sealed up the envelope so Mother could not check up on me and she tucked it in with the rest. I wondered if Auntie would tell, but she didn't. She's a peach.

Grandmother said she was sorry she had given me such an unwelcome gift.

I thanked her in a voice as sweet as the Turkish Delight that Mother used to buy in Toronto before sugar got so expensive. It was the sweetest thing I have ever tasted. We each got a stick of barley sugar today and it was lovely, but not as special as Turkish Delight.

I even said I would enjoy writing in the journal. I thought I was lying but maybe I wasn't. I am having a good time. If my hand was not growing tired, I could keep going for hours.

The journal is a nice one, as you could see if you were really here, with a ribbon to mark the spot where you left off writing. The pages are thick and creamy. You put the dates in yourself, too, so you can write lots on one day and skip the next, and it will still be fine.

So I can't get away with just doing the first few pages. Grandmother said she would inspect it next Christmas. I was in flat despair at the thought. But having you, dear Reader, changes everything. I can hardly believe how many pages I have already filled.

"Eliza, what are you up to?" Verity just asked me.

Ha ha! I've got her goat. It is a good thing the bed is wide or she'd be able to read over my shoulder.

"Just writing in my journal," I said, scribbling like mad.

She craned her neck, trying to get a peek, but I pulled it away and scowled at her. "You know, *don't* you, that journals are private property," I told her.

Now she is flustered. Good.

You are my age, dear Reader. You must be taller than I am. Almost everyone is. I am small for twelve. I have long dark flyaway hair. My nose is snub. Grandmother says, if I follow it, I'll end up in the right place. She's headed there too. Hers is positively pug. Girls in books almost always have beautiful eyes. But I don't want to talk about my eyes now except to say they are brown.

By the way, I have almost forgiven Verity. I heard Mother scolding her for being selfish and going off skating without me. "Mean-spirited" she called her. I could hear V. blubbering something about being tired of always having to be a big sister. She probably thinks I tattled, but I never did. It seems Father took in more than I thought he did when he found me sitting there with one boot off and one boot on.

The Duck who came to dinner turned out to be

Mrs. Mansefield, who is a widow. She said, in a mingy voice, that she was surprised to see the young people going out with skates on Our Lord's birthday. There was an awkward silence. Then Grandmother said, "I think they went out so I could have a quiet house for my afternoon nap. They are such thoughtful young people." "Oh," was all the Duck could say. Jack choked and had to be pounded on the back by Rufus. Grandmother is a brick.

Oh, good. Verity is putting her pen away. I will write another bit just to show her and then I will be free.

Good night, dear Reader.

Boxing Day

Tuesday, December 26

Last night, after we had turned off the lamp, I had the strangest thought. Jesus never had a chance to celebrate Christmas. Last year, it dawned on me that he did not speak English. I know this is true but I still do not quite believe it. I can't imagine him saying "Suffer the little children to come unto me" in Aramaic. That is the language Father says he spoke, Aramaic. Or was it Hebrew? I wonder what it sounded like. Anyway, he was a little boy once, as young as Charlie, and he never knew a thing about Christmas. I hope they celebrated birthdays at least.

Today we are all going skating, even Belle. Father is actually leaving the church to manage without him. *He* does not mind if I cling some of the time.

I wonder where Hugo is today and if he ever gets a chance to steal away from the War and go skating. They must skate in Europe. They surely do in Holland. You just have to remember *Hans Brinker or The Silver Skates.* I wonder what Hugo did for Christmas Day, and what kind of dinner he had. In their letters, they complain a lot about the food. But surely they will give the soldiers special food on Christmas Day! We don't get ice cream or cookies either, with sugar being so scarce, but we do get cottage pudding with last year's preserved fruit on top.

Now I will embark upon a description of the Bates family.

Mother and Father are the best of parents but they don't have much time to listen to me. Nobody has time for me.

I guess I should not blame them. It is not their fault that my brothers and sisters are all much older or much younger than I am. Hugo calls me Monkeyshines partly because I'm the monkey in the middle. Hugo is the eldest. He's my favourite. He joined up when the Germans sank the *Lusitania* in 1915. He was going to the University of Toronto, getting his B.A. He was twenty then. His birthday is on Valentine's Day.

Jack is next. He is nineteen now. He was going to the Agricultural College, hoping to farm. Mother's family owns a farm just outside Guelph where Aunt Martha and Grandmother live. Jack has always loved it there.

Then comes Verity Susan who is seventeen and thinks she is a Woman. I've already told you enough about her.

After her, comes myself, Eliza Mary.

If my twin sister had not died when she was just two months old, she and I would have been close companions. Grandmother told me that she was too frail to thrive, but Mother never speaks of her. Grandmother also said she was a perfect baby.

I wonder what sort of baby I was. Grandmother just smiled when I asked. I've seen some positively repulsive babies brought to be baptized. They improve later, usually, but at first they slobber and look like little red monkeys. Bald and bawling. I have seen a picture taken of myself when I was three weeks old. I was not bald. It is too bad you can't take coloured photographs. I am wearing a bib but no drool shows. I do not look ugly but blurry. That is all I can see for sure.

Next to me come the Twins, Charlie and Susannah. They are named after the Wesleys. (Mother was a Methodist before she married Father.) They are eight. I don't believe Susannah and Charlie are ever lonely the way I am. When the Twins were small they had a secret language nobody else could understand, but they finally started talking to the rest of us. Now that they go to school and have other friends it is a little better, but they are still as thick as thieves. Lots of times they know what the other one is thinking without saying a word. I suppose that is the way with twins.

I had a pretend friend called Posy Pretty when I was six, but she was too babyish. I really loved her when I was Belle's age, but she did not grow older with me the way a real friend would.

Belle, whose whole name is Emily Belle, is the baby. She turns five in a few days. She's supposed to be frail but Father says she's really as tough as an old boot. She has fair hair, silvery and bright, and huge deep blue eyes. Everyone spoils her but she stays sweet in spite of it.

So now you have met us all, dear Reader, the children of Sam and Annabelle Bates.

When I was coming inside earlier today I saw Cornelia at her window again and I waved harder, but she did not look up. She had on spectacles. Maybe she did not see me before. She must have been busy embroidering! I called her name but she still did not glance up.

I prick my finger when I sew and the seam gets lumpy and then either the thread tangles or breaks.

I don't mind really. I think sewing is tedious. Mother keeps threatening to buy me a sampler but she is not serious. Aunt Martha did one when she was little, but modern girls don't have time for such ladylike pursuits. Even Verity has not done one, although she has embroidered pillow shams for her hope chest. When I was about six or seven I imagined myself someday making a tapestry with flowers and deer and tall hound dogs, but I had not yet understood how I hate sewing. I had no notion they made those elegant pictures stitch by tiny stitch. I feel for all those court ladies. Father says they made them to help keep out the cold in those old castles, but I think I would have thought of some other way.

Wednesday, December 27

I got a postcard from Hugo today. He had a short leave in England before they start on some new push. He couldn't say what, of course. And he sent me a picture of the home of Charles Dickens, which he went to visit for my sake. Hugo is the best brother alive. He said nothing at all about the War except he hopes it will soon be over, but he doubts it. It *must* soon be over. It has lasted more than two years already and, in May, Hugo will have been gone two years. It feels like forever.

Mother and Father got a proper letter from him

and he said not to be anxious about him because he has had three narrow escapes and gotten away without a scratch. When the War ends, he promised, he'll come home with bells on and all in one piece.

"Amen," Father said.

I never thought before of your having a family, dear Reader, but you are becoming so real to me now that you must have relations to bless and beset you.

Mother told me once that, when she was twelve, she sometimes loathed Aunt Martha. I was flabbergasted. They seem to understand each other perfectly now.

We had a taffy pull too. My hands ended up sticky as a pot of flour paste, but sweeter. I wouldn't have spent so much time licking off flour paste. It wasn't just my hands either; I was taffy all the way to my elbows. Rufus made joking remarks but I did not let him get me riled. I was showing them how mature I could be but I don't think they noticed. It is very annoying when people notice your weak moments but never see your strong ones.

Thursday, December 28

I forgot to tell you that Father gave me my first fountain pen for Christmas. It's the prettiest green. It is so nice not to have to keep dipping the nib in the ink bottle or stopping to sharpen the pencil. I got my fingers inky when I was filling it, but I liked making it suck the ink up into itself. It makes a funny little noise like a mouse's hiccough.

I spent most of the day out-of-doors and all that fresh air has made me too sleepy to keep on writing, even to you.

Friday, December 29

On New Year's Day Jack and Rufus have to leave for England. Once they get there they're going to try to join the Royal Naval Air Service and defend England from the air. I have kept making myself forget, but now it is too close. Norah Sweet, Jack's girl, is coming to Uxbridge to visit on Saturday afternoon. They are not engaged, but everyone knows they plan to get married when the War ends. They are still too young, according to Mother and Father. She is so lovely to look at and she has a voice as soft as a cooing dove. Her eyes are big and velvety brown like pansies. Hugo did not seem to like her as much as the rest of us do, but everyone else thinks she is practically perfect.

Jack is excited about her coming. I can tell. Rufus keeps teasing him.

Saturday, December 30

Belle made the mistake of coughing just as we were about to go skating this afternoon. So Mother kept her home. The rest of us had a glorious time. True and Rufus were there as well as Verity and Jack, so they all got a chance to see me skate. I never went near them.

After we had been there quite a long time, Rufus came over, though, and asked me to skate with him. He is much taller than I am but we managed beautifully. We glided so smoothly.

He asked me about Norah.

"She is beautiful and Jack adores her," I told him. He will see for himself when she turns up. She was supposed to arrive last night but we have not heard from her. Maybe Jack has had some private word but has not told us.

Rufus changed the subject but he had sounded funny.

Jack thinks she is perfect. He sent her a fancy valentine last February. She showed it to me. He could not sign it, of course, but under the printed words he wrote, *I would swim the deepest ocean or climb the tallest mountain for you! Or even shinny up a beanstalk*. And he signed it, *The Giant Killer*. He's pretty smart, is Jack.

Norah has lovely eyes and silvery fair hair. But she does gush a bit. And she flutters her lashes. "Oh, Jack, you wouldn't!" she coos at him, gazing up, all flirty. This looks silly to me but Jack seems to eat it up.

Charlie teases him about his "lady love." He bats his lashes and pretends to swoon until Jack is in a right royal rage and then, just as Jack is about to trounce him, Charlie springs away like an antelope.

When we got home at last, Norah was sitting in front of the fire talking with Mother. I no sooner said hello than Mother sent me up here.

When I objected, she said, "Leave them alone, Eliza. It is the least we can do when they have so little time left."

But Norah could have come skating.

Later on they are going to a New Year's party where there will be dancing. They won't do it tomorrow night because it is the Sabbath. Jack and Father were arguing about this. Jack cannot see any harm in dancing and playing cards as long as you don't gamble or "go too far." I was glad Grandmother was out of earshot. She calls cards "the Devil's playthings." Mother says it is because people use them when they gamble.

Early afternoon, New Year's Eve

Sunday, December 31

Norah's aunt was at church this morning and she told Mother that Norah slept in. I did not think true love would sleep in when her sweetheart is going away to war tomorrow. But I have never been in love so I could be wrong. Maybe Norah needed her beauty sleep.

Rufus and Jack and a bunch of other young people went off to a big farewell party for the boys leaving for the Front.

I was standing at the door watching them go off down the street and Father came up behind me and looked out too. Then he said, under his breath, "Bring them safely home." I felt a shiver go right up my back. I ran upstairs to get away from whatever he might say next. Of course they will come safely home. How could they not? But I keep hearing Father's voice, so low, saying the words.

Was he talking to God? I suppose he must have been.

1917

Monday, January 1, 1917

Happy New Year, dear Reader! Or Happy Hogmanay, as Father said last night. He says we must not believe in foolish superstitions, but every New Year's Eve Hugo has gone out and been the young dark man who puts the "first foot" in the door and calls out, "Good luck and God's blessing on all in this house."

Nobody has ever asked Father if "first footing" is

a foolish superstition. He might just laugh, but he might be hurt somehow. He is strange about certain things.

New Year's dinner is not quite the same as Christmas dinner. For one thing, we always have goose. We do not have a haggis although my father always says we should. Haggis is not, in my opinion, a treat.

But New Year's dinner is a feast even now when there are shortages. I am not fond of being a minister's daughter except at times like New Year's. Father's parishioners bring him special treats. That is where the goose came from. Also the carrot pudding and the jar of mincemeat. And best of all, a box of fudge from old Mrs. MacDougall. She must have been saving up her butter and sugar for weeks. Maybe she begged some from her daughter in Toronto.

She handed me the box with a stern look and said, "Now, lassie, you make sure and certain the reverend gets his fair share of these sweets. I made them for him and not for a lot of greedy bairns to gobble up."

I took the box straight to him and hid some in the drawer of his desk where the Twins won't be likely to find them.

I told him what she said and he smiled but he still looked sad. The boys go on the afternoon train. It is hard to be really joyful today even sucking a great chunk of fudge.

After supper

We all went to the station to see the boys off. Jack and Rufus weren't the only men going. It was confusing. People were laughing and crying at the same time. Sweethearts were there, sobbing and hanging on to the men as though they would never let them go. Children dashed up and down the platform. Women held babies up to the train windows for one more kiss. Norah was gazing at Jack, getting ready for their last kiss. Then the train gave a toot and a big chuffing noise and pulled out of the station, leaving Norah puckering up for a kiss that never happened.

"Blow him one," Belle told her. "Hurry and blow him one, Norah."

For a split second Norah looked madder than a kicked cat. Then she smiled at my baby sister and blew a kiss after the vanishing train.

"He's blowing one back," Belle assured her in her shrill little voice that cuts through any hubbub.

Everyone was smiling by then and Norah had begun to blush.

"Belle has excellent eyesight," I told her.

She looked at me then. She did not smile. Then she walked away from us and joined up with a bunch of young people.

Poor Norah.

I secretly thought I would not miss Jack the way I missed Hugo when he left. But I do miss Jack. And I miss Rufus too with his red hair and big grin and his eyes that sparkle so when he is teasing.

Oh, dear Reader, let us both pray that 1917 finishes off the terrible War.

I still have not settled on a name for you. You will be more real with a name. I surely do like having someone to tell everything to. I can picture you reading all my adventures with baited breath. Maybe it is "bated" breath. Oh well, Reader, you know what I mean.

Grandmother and Aunt Martha took the next train into Toronto. They would have to change to go to Guelph. It was nice having them visit. But I am relieved that they are gone. If I told Mother that, she would scold, but I am certain she feels the same relief.

It is much, much quieter without those big boys and there is not nearly as much housework — but I wish they were back here, teasing but safe. Everyone cried when they left. Even Charlie blubbered a bit and had to pretend he had grit in his eye. I'm glad I am not a boy and can howl whenever I feel like it.

"Be a man, Charles," they tell him.

I don't see why he should. He is not nine yet.

Maybe it is not as wonderful as I used to think to be a boy.

Tuesday, January 2, 1917

How strange it feels to write 1917!

Let me tell you a little more about us and our manse, dear Reader. I left out a lot on Boxing Day and, since then, I've been so busy I forgot.

My father became the minister of Chalmers Presbyterian Church here in Uxbridge after the last minister dropped dead of a heart attack. Father had been in Guelph for years and was thinking of preaching for a call when he was asked to take over here. The manse is a brick house and most people would call it large. But our family fills every nook and cranny to bursting. It is a good thing, dear Reader, that you can sleep in a book instead of needing a bed.

Whenever someone makes a remark about seven children being too many for a poor clergyman, Mother points out that the Wesleys had nineteen and, if Mrs. Wesley had not kept at it, she would not have had Charles and we could never have sung Hark the Herald Angels Sing, or Love Divine, All Loves Excelling. I am sure you know that Charles was her *eighteenth* child — if you count them all. I am thankful that she does not mention that Mr. Wesley, like Father, was also named Sam.

I am even more thankful that my parents did not have eleven more children on the chance that the eighteenth would write wonderful hymns. Six brothers and sisters are more than ample.

The church ladies don't know where to look when Mother talks that way, but Father says he treasures her outrageous side, so that is that.

Maybe they don't care about singing as much as we do, but most of the best hymns seem to be written by Charles Wesley or Isaac Watts.

Mind you, Oh for a Thousand Tongues to Sing My Dear Redeemer's Praise always gives me the giggles. Imagine trying to sing anything with one thousand tongues in your mouth! Oh, I know it really means languages or people but it still tickles my funny-bone.

We are a musical family, dear Reader. On Sundays after we get home from evening service we gather around the piano and sing before bed. Sometimes some of the young people come over from church and join in. We often have a Duck or two still around. Singing seems to cheer them up. Even Miss Cadwallader who makes sheep's eyes at Father is not so bad when she is singing Fight the Good Fight With All Thy Might. Everyone gets to pick a favourite hymn. I love The Ninety and Nine because it tells a good story and Will Your Anchor Hold because it has such a great swing to it.

I am still amazed to be so enjoying writing this journal. I wonder what is different about me. I have suddenly become more interested in myself as though I am watching myself change into somebody else. I told Mother this and she said, "Well, Eliza, you *are* changing. You are beginning to outgrow little girl Eliza and starting to grow into Eliza, the young woman. Every day that passes, I am catching glimpses of her."

She was gazing at me in that significant way she has. It means she is telling me important news about myself.

I went red and stammered out something about not wanting to grow up yet.

Mother laughed. "Yes, you do, Eliza. Some of the time. It will grow easier. You'll see."

Dear Reader, does your mother say such things? I am only twelve.

I wish I could talk to Hugo about how strange I feel these days. I miss him so. When I was Belle's age I was terrified of the dark. I had to go to bed ahead of Verity, so I was all alone in our room for what seemed like *hours.* I would lie awake shivering. They all told me not to be foolish, but nothing helped. Then Hugo bought me a penny whistle. He showed me how to play it and told me to take it to bed with me because it was magic. "It will help you banish the dark," he said.

Then he taught me to sit up, face the part of the room which was darkest and play my whistle at it. Sure enough, the darkness seems to back away and grow thinner. You do not turn on a light. You look into the night and play a tune and all the fearful things melt away.

I keep it in the drawer with my ribbons and sashes and handkerchiefs now. I think I will get it out. When I pray for Hugo to be safe, I can send him a whistle. Jack told me that the soldiers cannot light candles or lanterns after dark because that would tell the enemy where to fire. I wonder if Hugo is ever afraid. He is so tall and gay. I cannot imagine him fearful.

Writing so much makes my hand ache. Yet I cannot stop. I think it is partly due to you, dear Reader, that I am liking journal keeping. Telling you things turns my life into a story like *Eight Cousins* or *Anne of Green Gables.*

Later

I am not one bit like Verity, thank Fortune.

"When you take up your diary," she said to me this morning, "you can record your New Year's Resolutions and then, next year, check to see if you carried them out."

Her tone said she knew I would fail but she thought it would be good for me to make the attempt. Verity is forever trying to reform me, but I am like Mother and I believe that Father treasures my outrageous side also.

"Why should I?" I asked her. "I'm perfect just the way I am."

Then I hummed a few bars of Just As I Am, Without One Plea to tease her. I thought she'd preach at me but, for once, she pretended not to hear.

She said I had better read hers so I would know what sort of thing to write. "My resolutions won't be at all like yours," I said. But I was curious. So I took her book and waited for her to leave the room. Finally she went. I am going to write down her resolutions so I can tease her when I catch her breaking one.

New Year's Resolutions
of Verity Susan Bates
January, 1917

Each one starts out "I resolve" so I'll skip that bit after the first one.

1. I resolve to tell the truth in these pages and to write in my diary every day.
2. to try to grow closer to Our Heavenly Father and to pray faithfully night and day.
3. to be a kind big sister and to set Eliza and the little ones a good example.
4. to write to Hugo, and Jack, and keep their spirits up as they fight for our country.

5. to help Mother with the housework and do so cheerfully.
6. to study harder so that I may be an informed wife and mother some day.
7. to practise the violin every day and not to mind the family's teasing.
8. to keep my clothes tidy.
9. to keep my temper.
10. to make my parents proud of me.

They sound just like Verity herself, stuffy and proper. She already keeps most of them. Her clothes are always tidy and she plays that dratted violin until I long to throw it on the floor and jump up and down on it. Yet, between you and me and the gatepost, I admit I am impressed. If she can do it, she will become a saint yet.

I will write more when I have found a completely private place in which to write to you, dear Reader. It isn't easy. I keep moving the journal from my pillow case to my bottom dresser drawer to under the bed. Yet I cannot risk leaving my journal where any of the family, especially Verity, could dip into it without my knowledge. You would think a minister's daughter could be counted on to be honourable at all times. Rubbish!

I vow I will *never* marry a minister. I don't want my children to bear the burden of being The

Preacher's Kids. Being such paragons is too much to ask — even of Verity.

Early Wednesday Morning

January 3

I did a dreadful thing. I wounded Verity. And I did it because of this very journal. I came into the room quietly, not wanting to wake her, and I caught her looking at my journal. Snooping! Nosey Parker.

I snatched it out of her hand and backed away. Then she smirked. She really did. I know it does not sound like something such a Goody Girl would do, but there is no other word for it. So I grabbed up my silver-backed mirror that Grandmother gave me when I was six and flung it at her head. She had turned away before I threw it, but she turned back. The handle caught her just above her left eye. Her alabaster brow, as Anne Shirley would say. It is bruised and swollen and I said I was sorry. But she had no right to pry into my private book.

Luckily the mirror landed on the carpet and did not break or I would have brought seven years of bad luck on myself.

Verity bawled like a newborn calf, of course. You would think I had run her through with a sword instead of merely giving her a knock on her noggin. Everyone came running. Nobody took my side.

Even Susannah looked shocked, as though she'd never seen blood shed before. That settles it. I will find a foolproof hiding place for my journal before I sleep tonight.

Later on

I forgot to mention that we are back at school. The teacher's name is Mr. Royle. He is forever giving some poor boy the strap. I am afraid of him. I liked my teacher in Guelph much better.

One of the girls' older brothers said that Mr. Royle was nicer before the War. Someone put a white feather on his desk last fall. They give those out to men who are too cowardly to enlist when their country needs them. Father says it is inhuman and he never wants to hear of one of us taking part in such a thing. As if we would! I don't like the teacher, but nobody should be humiliated, especially if he is really afraid. When Hugo gave me my penny whistle he told me that everyone is afraid at times, even the bravest of men. I wanted to ask if *he* had ever been really frightened but I didn't do it. Father is quite right about such questions being inhuman.

The boy laughed when he said Mr. Royle turned as white as the feather when he saw it lying there!

If men don't enlist, it doesn't *necessarily* mean

they're cowards. They won't take you if you have poor eyesight or flat feet or a bad heart. Mr. Royle wears thick glasses that make his eyes huge and frightening — they would keep him out of the army. After all, you have to see well to shoot straight. What if you shot one of your fellow soldiers by mistake!

The girls were right about my having to share a desk with Cornelia. She came back yesterday. But, after just one day, she got the sniffles and had to stay home again. When she plumped herself down next to me, she took up more than half the seat. It is not that she is so stout but that she wears so many layers of clothing. When we had to read, Mr. Royle skipped her as though she did not exist. I told her she had missed her turn.

"I don't have to do it," she said. "I'm too sensitive. My father told him. I have special problems."

If her eyes are bad, how on earth can she embroider night and day? I asked Father about it. He said Dr. Webb is a School Trustee and he also said not to tease Cornelia. I would not tease anybody. Well, I do tease my brothers and sisters, but that is different.

I found my private place for you, dear Reader, before we left for school. I am seated on the trunk my grandmother brought with her from Yorkshire. It is in the lumber room in the cellar. I am sure nobody but myself will come here. When I finish writing, I will hide the journal inside the trunk and take the key with me. No, I will hide the key down here too or I might lose it somewhere upstairs. I do lose things. There's enough light coming in through a small dusty window high in the wall above me and I brought candles in case it grows too dark.

Keeping this journal is so different. It will be easier to write about new things happening than just to keep writing about the same old things day after day. Even the War seems to keep repeating itself, as though the soldiers from each side were stuck on one bit of ground and they just keep fighting over it like dogs with a bone, only they aren't dogs. They are men killing other men, day after day. Mother has the saddest look on her face every time she reads the casualty lists in the newspaper, as if every name she reads is a son of hers. I have thought of hiding the paper but they would just hunt until they found it.

I just remembered what Verity said about resolutions. If I am going to write them, I should do it, but they will not be like hers. I should be filled with admiration for such a sister, but she is too good to be true. Hugo says she is training for sainthood. Presbyterians do not have saints, though, and I cannot imagine Verity becoming a Roman Catholic.

I am going to promise myself a couple of things but I will keep them simple. I will only write about things I want to write about and I will try to tell the truth and still make a good story out of it. That'll do.

I already told you about my eyes, didn't I? I don't care that my hair is straight or if I am too thin or anything, but I do wish I had no squint. None of the girls at school here has said anything yet in my hearing, but I know they will. I have heard them laughing about other girls and boys, Cornelia especially, in that secretive, gloating way mean girls have. They will get around to me. Maybe they already have. I don't care about them, but I do want more friends than just Cornelia.

Change the subject, Eliza Mary, or you will get tears on your journal.

I have told you a lot about the boys and Verity, dear Reader. Now I had better tell you more about Belle and the Twins, since I have not said too much about them so far. Susannah and Charlie were born on Christmas Day eight years ago. Mother said, "Father Christmas has a strange sense of humour. I asked for a new stove." My mother is fond of joking. We celebrate their birthday at the end of November. Christmas is too busy in a minister's house to add a double birthday into it. Then there is Belle, the baby, who turns five the day after tomorrow. She is a darling most of the time, although not always. She has been sick a lot and has terrible bilious attacks. She is very small for her age.

Having a minister for our father is not always easy but ours is better than most. Marjorie Leslie, who is also a preacher's child, cannot remember ever hearing her father laugh out loud or make a joke. In her house they never play games. He kisses their foreheads. And when they kneel by their chairs in the morning for family prayers, he tells God each little thing they have done wrong and asks for forgiveness for each one. All the Leslie children dread family prayers, dear Reader, and I do not blame them. We just fold our hands, close our eyes and bow our heads. I found out that Father and Mother used to kneel when they were first married and then she told him that she couldn't pray properly when her knees were aching so badly.

"He gave me a quizzical look," she said, "and the next day, we stayed on our chairs."

My father keeps family prayers much shorter and never mentions names except to ask for special blessings when someone is going away or writing a big examination or something. Now, of course, he prays for the boys, first ours and then all the rest. There are so many Uxbridge boys overseas. When he is not praying, he teases and tells funny stories. He says God wants us to have "merry hearts" and he can quote a Bible verse to prove it. Mother says he can quote scripture to prove anything. Grandmother says the Devil can quote scripture too. This is confusing.

Oh, I almost forgot Ezekiel, our parrot. My uncle

brought him from a pet shop as a present for Hugo's first birthday. They let him out of his cage and the first thing he did was bite Hugo's little finger. He still has a tiny scar. African Grey parrots are great talkers. Ezekiel actually swears. We did not teach him to. When there is a church meeting at the manse, we cover his cage. Sometimes he calls out things like "Moses and Aaron!" or "Jumping Jehosophat!" Once, when Mrs. Logan was visiting, Ezekiel said, "Holy haberdashery!" It is one of the expressions Father made up to take the place of swearing. When Uncle Jack bought him, he did not know that parrots can live to be eighty years old! He could still be around when Belle is an elderly lady.

Thursday, January 4

After I threw the mirror at her, and a bruise appeared, Verity started combing her bangs back so everyone would ask her how she had hurt herself. (She usually wears her hair in a bang which hides her eyebrows.) Mother saw me looking small this morning when one of the Ducks asked about it. After the old lady took herself off, my darling mother said, "You begged for that fringe of yours, Verity Susan. Now you either comb it down again, or I will personally cut it off. You know quite well that Eliza did not injure you on purpose."

Verity flounced off and came back with the bruise out of sight.

But I *did* do it on purpose, dear Reader. If you had told me the mirror would strike her, I still would have gone right ahead and let fly. Maybe I am a lost soul. I asked Father and he told me not to put on airs.

I wish I would get a whole letter from Hugo. I would like to receive one written just to me, but that is hard, I suppose, when you have to remember so many of us. In his last letter he put in, "Tell Monkeyshines that I miss her and I will be coming home soon to pull her pigtails." I wouldn't mind what he did as long as he came home safe and sound. He is a prince among brothers.

We are all waiting for the War to end. Father says it will not be soon, but the rest of us have higher hopes. When it started I remember people saying it would be "over by Christmas." Mr. Stephens from down the street offered to bet on it, but Father refused. He said later that Theodore Stephens was a fool. Father said wars are easy to start but hard to finish — like any other human quarrel. He is almost always right, but I hope he is wrong this once.

When it began, in 1914, it seemed very far away and unreal to me. I was just nine, after all, and I didn't even think about it unless an adult was talking about it. But now that my two big brothers have taken up arms and gone so far from home, I see things differently. It has grown much more real and even frightening. At times, it is thrilling. Then I remember how terrible it is, especially when I see Father and Mother worrying so. They try not to let it show when we are around, but I catch glimpses.

Later

I almost got caught. Just as I opened the cellar door, Big Sister spotted me. Her ears look exactly like question marks. I noticed it particularly.

"Where are you going?" said she.

I nearly shot back, "None of your beeswax," but stopped myself in time. Grandmother calls it a vulgar expression only used by vulgar people. Instead I stalked off with my nose in the air. I can see I may have to move my journal around the house from time to time. My sister is like Sherlock Holmes. Nothing escapes her once she begins wondering.

Cornelia Webb was back at school again. She is as white as a *blancmange* and her eyes are small and washed out. They remind me of some pale bluey-green marbles Charlie had once. I should not say one word about her eyes, though. After all, she does not have a squint like her seat mate. Maybe it is only her spectacles. She wears them in school when she struggles to read and she wears them when she sews. When she takes them off, her eyes water and she blinks all the time. Her eyes don't tell you anything about what she is feeling or thinking. They never laugh.

She is not friendly to me, but maybe she is shy. She is a year older than me even though she is in my class. When she had to recite, she stumbled over the simplest words and she was only saying "You Are Old, Father William." It practically recites itself.

When she got stuck and coughed, Mr. Royle let her off. His voice was snappish but she looked thankful. I think something is wrong with her.

Her family is Presbyterian but, for some reason, they no longer attend church. There are only three Webb children. Her house is so quiet that it is hard to believe there are people moving about inside it. In our house there is always noise, someone singing, the Twins and Belle scrapping, Father roaring "Who hid my spectacles?" or "Who took the newspaper?", Mother talking to herself, Verity practising her violin or elocution, Susannah or myself practising on the piano. Or Ezekiel, of course. He says things like, "Move along, sir." Or "Brush your hair, you bad girl." Jack taught him that.

But the Webbs are probably extra quiet right now because of worrying about Cornelia's brother, Richard. He was serving at the battle of the Somme. Father can scarcely speak about it. The Germans used mustard gas and our troops were not ready.

Father says mustard gas will be outlawed once people stop to think what they are doing, since it does terrible things to men who breathe it in. I had not thought about it until he told me this. It is evil because it attacks anyone who it reaches, a child, an animal, anyone. Also, if the wind shifts, it goes right back after the people who just fired it. If you are wearing your gas mask, I think you will not be killed, but men get careless when no gas attack comes for a while. A gas mask is hot and "damnably uncomfortable." I am quoting Father. And think of the horses and dogs!

Anyway, the Webbs' son Richard was at that battle and they have not heard from him in months. But he has not been reported as wounded or killed or taken prisoner. It must be terrible for them. I told Cornelia I was sorry but she just turned her head away and muttered, "*Don't* talk about it. Don't." And a few minutes later, she asked me to come over and play after school as if it were any old day and she had nothing on her mind.

I saw Mary Beth and Mabel smirking and whispering about us. I pretended not to be listening, but I think they meant me to hear. "Birds of a feather flock together," they were saying. And something like "Miss Google Eyes." I suppose they call Cornelia that because of her spectacles being so thick.

Dear Reader, I will confess I longed to turn my

back on her and run away and not go near her again. I am *not* like Cornelia Webb. She is not only peculiar in her appearance, she is backward. Think of being thirteen and still having trouble repeating "Father William." She is so stout too and her face has broken out in spots. I heard Mary Beth and Mabel singing "The Ballad of Lydia Pinkham" at recess. Everybody but Cornelia laughed. I don't think she understands that Mary Beth is mocking her.

Do you know the song, dear Reader? It goes:

Let us sing, let us sing of Lydia Pinkham.
A benefactress to the human race.
She invented her Vegetable Compound
And in the papers, they published her face.

The compound is supposed to cure everything, even pimples, but I don't think it works. Corny's are really bad and her father is a doctor, so he surely would get her some if it would do the trick.

The song goes on and on with funny verses, and Mary Beth and Mabel between them seem to know every one. Nobody looks at Cornelia. Wait until Mary Beth's face breaks out! I'll make up a new verse just for her.

How can they call Cornelia and me "birds of a feather"? We are not a bit the same. I am very good at reading and arithmetic and spelling too, not one bit like poor Corny.

Evening

When I got home from school Mother said that Richard has been officially reported as wounded. Maybe the other girls will be kinder to Cornelia now. Father went to pay a pastoral visit but was turned away at the door. Dr. Webb said, "There is no God, sir."

I would have been furious, but Father feels pity for him. I heard him telling Mother that the man looked eaten up with despair.

Friday, January 5

Belle turned five today. When she first got up we said, "Happy Birthday, Belle," and she said "Happy Birthday" back to us. It was hard not to laugh at her. She's quaint. At breakfast she suddenly said, "When will I be five?" We all stared at her. "You are five now," Father said, smiling. "*Now!*" said Belle. "You mean, I am five right this minute?" "That's *it*, you silly baby," Charlie grinned. She looked down her tiny nose at him. "Five-year-olds are *not* babies, Charlie," she said. "I can write my whole name and Mother said you could not do as well when you were my age."

Everyone laughed and Charlie blushed. She is so different from the Twins. (Mother calls them the rowdy rapscallions.) Most of the time Belle is serious and sweet. Her eyes are so round and blue and solemn. Her hair is so fair it is almost white and it curls all over her head. Hugo calls it her "halo." (Susannah's hair is chestnut. It is always in a wild tangle. Charlie's matches except it is shorter, of course.)

Verity and I put our Christmas money together to buy Belle a doll for her birthday. She has named her Belle Anna after herself and Mother. She nurses her as if she were a live baby, and can hardly leave her long enough to eat.

At first Verity thought we should give her a book of Children's Prayers. Can you believe it? It is the sort of gift you expect from your great aunt. "Belle would rather play than pray, and you know it," I said. My big sister actually laughed and gave in at once. Maybe she was just teasing me. But I do not think so. Verity is not a tease. She does not even get other people's jokes, let alone making any herself. Even when you have explained a joke to her, she just gazes at you and says, "Oh," in a voice that tells you she does not understand at all. I can't imagine being like that. It must feel like not being able to taste food or having no ear for music. It must feel, dear Reader, as if everyone else spoke one language and you just knew enough of it to get by.

Thank goodness all the birthdays are over until spring. I am as poor as a church mouse. I suppose in any family of seven children, birthdays are going to clump together sometimes, but so many right at Christmas are hard to finance.

Saturday, January 6

Nothing much happened yesterday. The War news must have been bad because Father ate his scalloped potatoes without a word. He usually complains when we have them. He calls them "sloppy" and mutters about the roast potatoes his mother made. Mother never gets them right.

Moppy came back from visiting her family over New Year's. I should have mentioned her since she has lived with us ever since I can remember. She came to work for Mother when the Twins were born and she has never left. Her real name is Miss Constance Miller, but she is always mopping or sweeping and she ended up being called Moppy. Even Father calls her that. Grandmother, when she comes, does not. She says Miss Miller. Moppy scolds us, but everything is easier when she is here because Mother does not have to do all the housework herself and Verity and I don't feel so guilty when we forget to lend our hands. Mother never has to remind Moppy to use elbow grease and make the dirt fly. She does it automatically.

It is nice to be back at school but it is also nice to have the weekend free.

Also I finished *Eight Cousins* and Mother gave me *Rose in Bloom* as a surprise. I don't like it quite as well. I loved it when Rose was being surprised by everybody.

Sunday, January 7

When Father prayed for the families of all those fighting in the War or suffering because of it, and did *not* pray that the Kaiser get struck down with lightning or something worse, I could feel the congregation tightening their mouths and giving him cold looks. I wish he would pray for God to be on our side and for us to *win*. The Germans are such vile beasts, killing those Belgian babies and sinking the *Lusitania* and using mustard gas. Father wanted Hugo to stay in school and wait until he was older before he joined up, but the day the news came about the sinking of the *Lusitania*, Hugo went straight to the recruitment office to enlist.

I remember when we first heard about the Germans sinking the *Lusitania*. That was a terrible day. So many little children were on that ship. Susannah dreamed about them and woke us all up screaming that they were in the dark water holding out their arms to her and begging her to save them. After she sobbed it all out, I was afraid to shut my eyes in case I had the same dream, but I think Susannah is more sensitive or something, because I never did.

Charlie says that a boy at school said that the Germans toasted babies alive and ate them. Father got extremely angry and roared at him that Germans are mostly just ordinary people like us. I don't understand how he can say such a thing. He says war is wicked. He is right, of course, but we did not start this wicked war. I am proud of our soldiers. They are so brave and handsome when they march past with the bands playing "Rule Britannia." The Twins stand at attention and salute and I do too. Two weeks ago we were singing Onward, Christian Soldiers and, all at once, I had to blink hard to keep back the tears. Knowing real soldiers were marching off to a real war, where there are real shells and people getting wounded, changes the feeling of the song. Before it was just a jolly march. Now it is not jolly at all.

Yet it still has a grand sound.

War is confusing. One minute you are excited. The flags are flying and the march music makes you stride out. You can feel your eyes sparkle and your arms swing to the thumping of the drums or the drone of the bagpipes. (Father says the right word is "skirl" but I am not so sure and this is *my* journal.) Then you hear about the wounded men and you see the lists of missing and dead. I cannot understand how it can all be part of the same thing. Why were

Hugo and Jack in such a hurry to go, as if it were all a huge adventure, when it might end so terribly? Is it the flags flying and the band music and the uniforms? God could not let anything terrible happen to Hugo or Jack or Rufus. He won't.

Monday, January 8

Once again, Verity caught me — almost. I heard her calling my name from the top of the stairs and I froze, hardly breathing, waiting for her to leave. Trust Verity Susan Bates not to give up that easily. When I heard her starting down I flung myself into the coal cellar. It is so dark and dirty in there that I thought I'd be safe. I thought she would think she heard rats. She is terrified of them and Charlie teases her by saying he has seen them down here. It worked. But after she gave up searching and I came out, I found I was covered with coal dust. I looked like Tom in *The Water Babies* after he's been sweeping chimneys. I was at a loss what to do. Thank goodness I had had enough sense to bundle the journal up in my skirt and it was not badly smudged. I hid it away, holding it with my petticoat, and then crept up the stairs to listen. There was no sound. I ran back down and went out the cellar door and through the hedge to Cornelia's.

I knocked and then walked in quick. How Mrs.

Webb shrieked when she saw me! But they actually helped me have a bath. They have indoor plumbing. They have *two* bathrooms! We have one and ten people to use it. That is why we still use the privy during the day. They have hot water coming to both bathrooms. At our house, more than one person uses the same water and, if we want it hotter, we heat up the big kettle on the woodstove and add it. We take turns too and you have to go in order. Saturday Bath Night is a Shakespearian extravaganza with "its exits and its entrances." Father said that. What luxury at the Webbs! And they ran the tub half-full just for me. They don't use Lifebuoy at the Webbs' for all it is supposed to be so healthy. Their soap smells of lavender.

I borrowed clean clothes from Cornelia. She has a dress almost the twin of my brown flannel and it hangs loosely so it does not matter that I am thinner. And Mrs. Webb is going to return my clothes to me in secret. She is a real brick! I wonder what my mother would have done if Cornelia had gotten black with soot and fled to her for help. I could not explain I was hiding from Verity, but they seemed to guess. They never asked awkward questions. Best of all, True was out and missed the whole thing. She has become such a bosom friend of Verity's that she would have told, you can bet your bottom dollar.

I am going to make a cover for this journal so Verity cannot see what book it is, and then I can write in it more openly. I found some oilcloth I can use. I got Moppy to say she'd make me a book cover and not tell anyone. I have to help with the dishes without complaining for a month. It is a lot to ask. I so enjoy complaining.

Tuesday, January 9

The Webbs have had more news about Richard. (I should have mentioned it before.) He is in hospital in England. Cornelia's father has gone over to see him. He is a surgeon so they might let him bring Richard home. I don't know what exactly is the matter with him. He is not blind, though, and he has not lost an arm or leg. Susannah asked. I was embarrassed but also glad to know. Children come in handy sometimes.

Moppy told me today that she can see my grown-up self in my face sometimes now, and she thinks I may be a lovely looking woman. I think she is trying to comfort me for my straight hair and eye trouble, but maybe I am wrong. Look at Anne Shirley. Her hair turned auburn by the time she went to college.

My brown hair may grow darker. I would like it to be dramatic like Belle's or Rufus's. Not much chance, I fear.

Mother says I must help with the war effort now

I am twelve. I was pleased until I found out she is going to make me learn to knit socks! I feel all thumbs when I knit. And I cannot pick up stitches when I drop them. Mother says I just have to keep my mind on what I'm doing and not go off into a brown study. But she has a plan which may make all the difference. One person will read aloud while a bunch of us knit. Maybe I could be the one who does the reading.

Thursday, January 11

The war news must be bad again. Father looks sad and Mother is pale and anxious. Father has a big map of Europe in his study and he has little coloured pins marking the troop movements he reads about in the newspaper. There are pins marking where battles have been fought — the Somme, Festubert, Givenchy, St. Eloi — names I never knew before the War.

It seems so far away. If we knew where the boys were, it would be different. Verity listens to every word the adults say as though she understands, but I think she is just being a good daughter the way she said in her resolution.

I had to go to Prayer Meeting tonight. Children don't go but Mother says I am no longer a child. I yearn to be older at times, but not when it comes to Prayer Meeting. Two women bring their knitting to church but Mother does not approve. I think she thinks they are showing off. I watch them and they don't ever look up when Father says something surprising. Mrs. Thorpe does not shut her eyes when Father prays either. I told Mother. "How would you know that, my dear Eliza?" she asked in a teasing voice. Just in time, I realized what I was about to confess. "I noticed just as I was closing mine," I said quick as a flash.

"She must have closed hers one second later," Mother said. "Old people's eyelids move more slowly, you know."

Then she laughed out loud, something she does not do often lately. I felt pleased with myself.

Saturday, January 20

The Bates family has a dog! We cannot believe it. We have begged for one for years. I never thought Mother would agree to such a thing. Susannah came screaming in to tell us some big boys were drowning a puppy in the horse trough at the corner and Belle might get killed saving it. Charlie took off like a bolt of lightning. I ran after him. Susannah and I got there just in time to help Charlie and Belle and little Ellie James from Belle's Sunday school class beat off the boys and haul the puppy out of the freezing water. They had smashed the crust of ice and were plunging him in headfirst when Belle saw them. She screamed to Susannah who was out sweeping the snow off the front porch and then raced to start the rescue. For a little girl who is supposed to be frail, she fights like a tiger.

It was Belle, of course, who finally talked Mother around. When she and Charlie brought the puppy in, dripping ice and blood from scrapes, and limp with shock, I didn't have to put in my two cents worth. Charlie's battered appearance worked wonders. And poor Belle was blue with cold and shaking with outrage and misery.

"How could they?" she kept crying. "How could anyone?"

It would have taken an inhuman person to look into her big wounded eyes and say, "Put the little beast outside and let it take its chance." Mother is entirely human.

Our hero Charlie has a cut lip and two black eyes, and the dog, whose name has yet to be decided, has no deep cuts but is battered and bruised. We thought he might die at first, dear Reader. He just lay there and shook and shivered. But he is like Belle, tougher than he looks. He has recovered his spirit. He's full of true grit and he's comical looking. One of his ears stands up and one falls down. He has a circular whip of a tail which has a double curl when he is happy. He carries it high over his back. But, dear

Reader, between you and me and the gatepost, the tail itself is terribly skinny and, except for the curl, not impressive. It can wag so fast, though, that it is almost a blur.

An hour later

His name is Isaac.

Mother called him that because she had maintained for twenty-three years that she would not have a dog and now the Lord has sent her one. She says she feels like Sarah in the Bible, who was so old when she found out she was going to have a baby that she burst out laughing. Isaac means laughter.

"Your mother is irreverent, but that is certainly a laughable dog," Father said.

Isaac adores Mother. He knows where the little treats will come from.

Susannah says it's a perfect name because that Bible Isaac was almost killed and then was saved by a kid. "Charlie is a kid," she pointed out.

Of all the Bible stories, that is the one I hate. I asked Father if he would sacrifice me if God told him to. He said his God would never tell him to do such a daft thing.

Then he saw he had hurt my feelings so he said quickly, "God knows I could not manage without my Eliza."

Father is good at wiggling out of theological discussions. Now he has announced our dog is named after Isaac Watts, which is only fair after all the family emphasis on the Wesleys. (Except for Jack, of course, who was named after John Knox, John Calvin and John Wesley.) Jack is "short for" John but it doesn't make sense because John is just as short. I asked Mother if she knew why.

"It has been that way forever. Little Jack Horner was an abbott whose real name was John. It is just the way it is," she said.

I don't like explanations that don't explain a thing, but once you get started on names, there seems to be no sense to it. Hugo, by the way, is named after one of Father's boyhood friends.

Isaac is a dear little dog and he cheers us all up. Hugo will love him. I'll write him the whole story in a letter tonight before we go to bed.

Friday, January 26

Dr. Webb has seen Richard. He is shell-shocked and gassed. His nerves have broken down and he is in "a deplorable state." That is what Mother heard from Mrs. Webb.

"She couldn't say more," Mother told Father.

Mrs. Webb must be like Cornelia. I did not like to ask her what that part about "nerves broken down" means exactly. I already know Cornelia does not like talking about anything too real. She would not even look at Isaac until he became presentable and healed up. Belle told me she was there that day and saw the boys and just ran away. We have never mentioned it. But if Isaac upset her that much, talking about Richard would upset her dreadfully.

True talked to Verity but she had nothing new to add. They are going to let Dr. Webb bring Richard home. I wonder what he will be like. Charlie thinks he will have stories of battles to tell, but Father says he is not to ask Richard for stories.

"He will be in no condition to spin yarns," Father began. "Poison gas is evil." Then he sounded as if he might cry and went into his study and shut the door hard. Susannah said she did see tears in his eyes. He did not come out for ages.

We have started the Knitting Group. We are reading *A Tale of Two Cities.* Mother says I can read aloud once I finish my first sock. I fear that means I won't read a word of this book. It is exciting and so sad. When we're at the group, I keep forgetting to knit. Mother reminds me, but once I saw her needles stop as she gazed into space, and her lips were trembling. I knew that she was not in our parlour. She was in the Paris prison with Charles Darnay. I reached out to poke her and then did not do it. I am more merciful than she.

We all got playing with Isaac tonight, and Belle's Eaton's Beauty Doll got left outdoors. She looks dreadful. Belle keeps singing, "I once had a sweet little doll, dears," in a mournful voice, hugging the faded child close. I could not help laughing to myself, but I kept her from seeing. Does my laughing mean I am turning into an adult who does not understand the broken heart of her little sister? I hope not.

Sunday, January 28

The house is so cold these days. I get under my covers and keep even my head buried and still the bitter wind sneaks in after me. The church was cold, of course. I told Mother that we should bring in our blankets that we use in the carriage and wrap them around our legs in church. She said she understood my feelings, but I clearly had no sense of the fitness of things.

We stayed in the kitchen close around the woodstove until bedtime. Once we get under the covers, Verity and I make ourselves into spoons to keep warm. Too bad Isaac will not sleep with us, but he cannot be won away from Belle.

Cornelia Webb came over to play yesterday. I think she likes to get away from her quiet house and her sad mother so I don't ask about her brother.

They have had no more news or, if they have, they have not told poor Cornelia.

She is now so much friendlier, but she is certainly not adventuresome. She likes to play with paper dolls better than anything. We cut them out of the catalogue and old fashion magazines her mother gets. I like naming them and deciding who belongs in what family but it is the clothes that Cornelia likes. She has lots more dresses than I do. (That stands to reason considering the number of children needing clothes in our family.) I mostly wear middy blouses, but she wears proper dresses even to school.

It is fortunate that I like middy blouses. They are more comfortable than most other clothes. Maybe they make me feel as free as the boys. Often I wish we could wear trousers. Boys never get told to keep their knees together and sit like ladies. But some girls, like Cornelia, don't mind.

I asked her what she wants to be when she grows up. She just stared at me goggle-eyed.

"A wife and a mother, of course," she said. "I'd like to have four children, twin boys first and then twin girls."

I thought of telling her the amount of work our twins were when they were babies, but let it go. "We could be nurses or teachers," I said, "and then be wives later."

"No," she said. "I won't need to do that. My father will support me until I get married. He does not approve of women working outside the home."

I gave up, dear Reader. She is without an ounce of ambition or imagination. They have a woman who comes to do their laundry. She is a widow with a big family like Mrs. Ruggles in *The Birds' Christmas Carol.* I wanted to ask Cornelia if her father approved of that lady, but I knew it would be rude and it would probably make her confused.

When Cornelia told me she would have four children, I suddenly felt a lump in my throat. Who would marry poor Cornelia? Maybe nobody will want to marry me either, but I will be happy being either a nurse or a teacher. I can't make up my own mind. I think I might be a good teacher.

You could not become a teacher without being able to read well. When I told Cornelia my plan, she shuddered. I should say "my dream," dear Reader. It isn't a plan quite.

Thursday, February 8

Richard Webb was brought home today. The hospital wanted to keep him longer, but he got so upset that they decided he would be better with his family, since his father is a surgeon. He has an office in town. Cornelia says their house here in Uxbridge was Mrs. Webb's before she married, and was not suitable for an office.

Richard came while we were home for our dinner at noon. From the dining room window we saw him being helped into the house, and he has not come out even once. I asked Moppy.

"Poor soul," she said and wiped tears from her eyes.

Cornelia stayed home from school. I saw her afterwards and asked her how he was, but she ran into the house without saying a word.

Verity took some fresh bread over to them though, and got herself invited in. She actually saw him. Trust her for that! She said he did not speak while she was there, but True tells her he stammers terribly and twitches. Dr. Webb told them that Richard has nightmares which make him scream. He dreams he's back in the trenches and is buried alive and keeps begging someone to get him out.

We got a letter from Hugo the other day telling us about their trench cat. They do have animals there. This cat of Hugo's walked into their outpost one night and never left. They call him Scrounger and he seems to have a charmed life. He has only lost a tiny bit of one ear even though he has been on hand when shells were bursting. Some men even have pet rats.

The stories Hugo tells sound so much more

cheerful than the things True said about Richard. I am afraid that means Hugo skips the worst parts to shield us. I wonder if lots of them do the same. I don't want to be shielded and yet, I do, if it is too terrible to be borne.

Cornelia's silence is easier to understand now. She must be terribly muddled by Richard's acting the way True told Verity. Maybe she just can't bear to see hurting things. She needs life placid. Poor Cornelia. From what I've seen and from the news of the War, life is not going to be placid in our world and we must take courage and be strong.

Friday, February 9

I saw Richard Webb today. I never met him when he was well, of course. I think he was handsome once. But his face is grey and it keeps grimacing as though he is in terrible pain. He shivers and he stammers. Sometimes he shouts out words, and now and then he whispers, as though he is afraid someone is listening.

He was out in their back garden for a few minutes this afternoon but they took him in again when he started to shout. I could not help but see since the Twins and I were shovelling the snow off our garden paths. He really frightened me. I felt like running inside and slamming the door. But I did not do it.

I didn't look straight at him and I warned the Twins not to stare. "What is wrong with him?" Susannah blurted out. She has a loud voice, very deep. I tried to hush her but she would not listen to me. She asked if he was a lunatic. I told her to be quiet and I said he was sick. "No. The child is right," he roared out. "I'm a maniac. A loony." Charlie giggled. He was nervous, I think. Then Richard began to cry.

Father must have been listening. He came out the back door, passed us and went through the gate in the hedge.

"Let me help you back into the house, Mr. Webb," he said so gently that my eyes filled with tears. "It is too cold for you out here."

"Don't touch me," Richard screamed. Then he stumbled toward the door.

Father followed him, making sure he got in safely. Mrs. Webb met them on the step and thanked Father. I was going to ask him about Richard when he came back, but he went out their garden walk to the street and did not return to where we were. The Twins wanted to stop working right then and run after him to ask what had happened, but I held them back, telling them Father would be helped more by the shovelling being done than by a lot of questions. I knew by the look of his back striding off that he wanted to be alone.

I know, dear Reader. Backs cannot stride off — but you know exactly what I mean.

I am sure I have already told you that Father does not believe in war. He is in trouble about it because he will not pray for God to give the Kaiser boils or leprosy or some other deadly plague. He does pray for our fighting men, asking God to bless them and keep them safe. But he prays for both sides to come to their senses.

The head of Session told Mother today that when the last minister died suddenly and Father preached for the call, the congregation took it for granted that he was truly patriotic because they had heard about Hugo being at the Front. They were deeply shocked to find Father so peace-loving "at an hour when our Whole Civilization is in Peril." Mother told Father what she heard the Elder say, and Father said, "That man talks only in capital letters." He laughed, but he sounded unhappy. Then he said, "He'd hand *me* a white feather if he did not know they would not take me."

I came to find you, dear Reader, since I should not listen in on them. I do it anyway, but I suppose I should not.

It is strange to think that Hugo's going to war might have gotten Father the call to this church. When Hugo came home in uniform, he asked Father to forgive him. Father hugged him and could not say one word. The Twins cheered and I saw Verity looking at him as if he were a god. Like Apollo or one of those Greek ones. Do I mean Hercules? I get them mixed up.

I think he looks wonderful in his uniform. Jack and Rufus will too, especially once they get their Royal Naval Air Service uniforms. Jack can't wait to put on the navy blue with its gold buttons. I am so proud of them, dear Reader. Besotted, Father says when he gets teasing me. Do you have a brother in uniform? Somehow I think you are an only child.

I am afraid for Hugo, as well as proud, but I struggle not to think about it.

Dear Father in Heaven, do not let anything terrible happen to Hugo. He is so strong and brave and jolly. I pray this in Jesus' name, Amen.

I went out on the verandah a few minutes ago to see the stars. I heard Richard W. screaming at his mother as though he did not know who she was. Then Cornelia shouted out, "Make him be quiet. Make him stop." She can't talk about him without crying. Yesterday she shocked me by bursting out that he had spoiled everything by coming home. She saw the look on my face and she ran away from me and we haven't spoken properly since. How could you be angry at your own brother who is so hurt? I know I decided she was weak and could not help being that way, but she still shocks me. I cannot understand her. If Hugo came home like that, I would cherish him every moment.

Mother brought me a new library book called *Rebecca of Sunnybrook Farm*. She says I am like Rebecca. Rebecca reminds me of Anne Shirley but I like Anne better. Or maybe it isn't Anne herself I like better but the rest of the story. Rebecca isn't as harum-scarum and she is not an orphan.

After I thanked her for the book, I told Mother about Cornelia hating reading. She's nearly fourteen and cannot read even the easy words. And I told her about what Corny said about Richard spoiling things.

Mother looked sad. "Be thankful for your good mind, Eliza," she said. She told me that Mrs. Webb is worried about Cornelia. She was very ill as a baby. She had several convulsions and, although she pulled through, she has always been slower to do things than other children her age. "Perhaps I shouldn't talk to you about her like this," Mother said, "but I think she needs your understanding. Her father keeps punishing her for not working harder at her lessons."

I stared at her. I couldn't believe she was telling me this, but she even went on.

"He says she just does not apply herself. But her mother and I believe she does the best she can. It is hard on her having True for a sister, and Richard was always top of his class before he enlisted."

"Oh, my," I said. I could not think of anything else.

"That family has had more than its share of troubles," Mother said.

Then, dear Reader, she went and added, "I'm glad Cornelia has you for a friend, Eliza."

I like it when she talks to me as though I were an adult but, to be honest, I am not such good friends with Cornelia. I'm too old for paper dolls and I hate sewing. When I try to get her to come out for a walk, she's always too tired or she dawdles. It is no fun walking with a dawdler. But I will try harder. Sigh!

Monday, February 19

I know. I have neglected you, dear Reader. But I have been so busy with schoolwork and knitting and writing letters overseas. But here I am again, for I have something interesting to tell.

Richard Webb hardly sleeps. We can hear him shouting and moaning until his father gives him a sleeping draught.

"The poor laddie," Mother murmurs.

Cornelia stayed home from school again. But when I came in, she was sitting in our kitchen with a face like stone. When I stared at her in astonishment, she jumped up and ran out the door.

"You be gentle with that child, Eliza," Moppy said, as though I had been planning to be cruel to her, which I was not.

I snapped that I couldn't be gentle if she never lets me come close.

"You keep trying," was all she answered. Why was Cornelia in our kitchen? Getting away from her brother, I suppose.

Or perhaps it was her shame at getting not one right answer on her arithmetic test last week — and Mr. Royle gave her the questions he gives to the ten-year-olds. It would not be so bad if he didn't talk to her about it out loud where everyone could hear.

Thursday, March 1

I know. I have missed a few days again, dear Reader. I forgot about you because we have been working on a school pageant. I will be the Spirit of England. My costume is mostly a Union Jack made into a dress, and a crown and sceptre which are used for every play with a king or queen in it. Even Herod holds them in the Christmas play. I think I look silly but Mabel looks worst as the Spirit of France with lilies all over her and a big ribbon crossing her front. The ribbon is too short and she looks ridiculous bulging over it.

Cornelia is at home with grippe again. Her father never treats her the way a doctor father should. You would think she made her nose run on purpose to annoy him. "Where is your handkerchief, young lady?" he asks in such a sharp voice. "Please employ it."

She looks scared when he talks straight to her and glares. My mother got her a bottle of Aspirins. Her father says she does not need pills, just mustard plasters. But these Aspirins really help her head not to ache and Mother says they are better for her than laudanum.

I cannot imagine being afraid of Father. But Dr. Webb barks at Cornelia in such a fierce way, as though she is an utter dunce and he is ashamed of her. When I was there yesterday, even Richard noticed.

"Stop it, stop it, stop it, sir!" he yelled. Then he saluted his father and hid under the table.

I wished I was anywhere but there.

But I also wish that Cornelia would not snuffle like that. She sounds a little like a pig. I can tell you such unkind things, dear Reader, which is a relief. Sometimes I fear I am more of a beast than Verity.

At school today Mabel showed us an item from the newspaper about the battalion her cousin is in, the 116th. They are going to the Front. Colonel Sharpe said in the paper that when he told the men they were going to France as a unit, "you could hear their cheers for two miles."

Bedtime

A letter came from Hugo. He didn't send anyone a message. Whatever he did say made Mother cry. I think somebody from where we used to live must have been killed. I told Mother I was old enough to know, so she gave me the news at last. Ross Maynard was not killed, but he has had to have his right leg amputated. Hugo helped get him to a stretcher and he said Ross kept asking for his mother.

I wish I did not know. Ross is older than Hugo and I never really knew him. But I do remember one thing about him. He was a wonderful runner. He used to win all the foot races at school.

Father says we must pray for the wounded. I think we should have prayed earlier. But I'm beginning to wonder if praying does any good.

Ross Maynard has a brother who is Verity's age. He must be sick at heart. If they bring him home, will his brother feel like Cornelia does about Richard? Never.

They did not tell the Twins yet. Mother told me not to talk about it where they could hear. Then she made a big pan of Russian toffee to send to Hugo. Moppy has knitted more socks too. Hugo says her socks have saved him and his friends from frostbite. He says it is terribly cold at the Front. She knits them fast as lightning and sends them in bundles and he passes them out. They love the Russian toffee because it does not get hard but stays all fudgey.

Mother has finally given up on my ever completing a sock which could be worn by a human foot. When the knitters meet, I'm always the one who reads aloud now. We're still on *A Tale of Two Cities*. Mother asked the Webbs to join us, and Cornelia knits faster than her mother or True. She never drops a stitch. And her whole face looks different, as though she's really alive in a way she usually is not.

It is wonderful to sit and read a great book without feeling guilty. Almost always, you have to steal reading time.

I look over to see if Cornelia is listening to the story. I don't think she is. But she isn't minding. Even Madame Defarge does not make her shudder.

Friday, March 2

Susannah is very proud of herself tonight. This morning she spelled down all the boys in the class Spelling Bee. She spelled the girls down too, but the boys seem to be the ones that matter. The words that defeated the last two boys were *parallelogram* and *hypotenuse*. I am glad she didn't ask me to spell them. She asked Father. She should have known he would get them right without even needing to stop and think.

Charlie said he could spell *Mississippi* so Father told him to prove it.

"Missississississ . . . " Charlie started in. When he saw us beginning to laugh, he yelled out, "ippy."

We laughed so hard he stamped off up to his room and would not come back even for the last of the peaches Mother and Moppy put up last summer. Because there's so little sugar or proper flour to be had, Moppy makes wartime cottage pudding, which she herself says tastes like sawdust, and then we spoon the peaches over it. It is not delicious, but it is usually good enough to tempt Charlie. We all felt mean. Susannah forgot he had been teasing her and looked at us as though we were monsters. She would not eat dessert either. She took Isaac and went upstairs to look in on Charlie. Half an hour later, I saw Moppy carrying up a big bowl filled with dessert, twice the peaches the rest of us got. I'll have to practise making spelling mistakes!

Wednesday, March 7

There has been a revolution going on in Russia. Some of the Session Elders were here and they could talk of nothing else. The Czar may even have to give up his throne. Father is unhappy about the whole situation in Russia. When I asked him why, he said I would not understand unless I knew how the Russian peasants have lived for years, and that he would give me a book to read.

"Not *War and Peace*," Mother said. "I know Eliza is a great reader, Sam, but there are limits."

It was *War and Peace*. It comes in two volumes and it is enormous, but I will try. I am proud Father thinks I can do it. Mother told me not to be afraid to skip if I got bogged down. She says all the parts about Natasha I would like, but she was not sure I would take to Napoleon. She helped me figure out their names. Each of them has a whole bunch which sound not at all the same.

Soon it will be spring and maybe soon the War will end. We have to plough up the earth and plant vegetables for our garden, so we can be more self-sufficient. But that is a while away yet.

The Missionary Society are putting on a concert to raise money for the War. People in Toronto have already raised enough money to provide a whole hospital ship. And mothers whose husbands are away at war need help, too. Father has suggested that Verity and I perform a dialogue. She takes elocution lessons and recites poems making grand gestures. I secretly think she looks silly and poems don't need all that hand waving and clutching the heart. The elocution teacher even rolls her eyes up to show woe or surprise or something. I opened my mouth to say "No!" but Verity beat me to it. She has already agreed to do "Abou Ben Adam" by Leigh Hunt.

Mrs. Macdonald, who wrote *Anne of Green Gables* under her maiden name of Lucy Maud Montgomery, is a great reciter and she works for the Red Cross and knits. She is the Presbyterian minister's wife at Leaskdale, which is near Uxbridge, so we see her now and again. Mother says we must invite them to dinner but she has not done it yet. I know she is nice because I have read all her books, but she is not like Anne Shirley. Maybe it is because she is married to a minister. I have a feeling Father and Mr. Macdonald are not kindred spirits by the way Father's voice changes when he speaks of him.

I never told you what a success the school pageant was. Mabel's sash fell off right in the middle of her big speech. I did not laugh but it was a struggle.

Thursday, March 8

The strangest thing happened. I feel I must write about it and yet perhaps I should not. Perhaps I was wrong about what I thought. Mother had gone to the store today and they had a tiny drop in the price of beef, so she got some for us and for the Webbs too. She sent me over with it. Nobody seemed to be home so I just went in quietly to put it in the icebox. When I got to the kitchen I was so startled I dropped the package. Richard was standing beside the sink with a paring knife in his hand. He had his sleeve rolled up, and he was shaking like a poplar leaf.

"What are you doing?" I stammered. "You'll cut yourself."

I know, dear Reader. It was stupid. But I could not think of anything else to say. He dropped the knife with a clatter and lunged around and glared at me. His eyes were so wild!

"What if I do?" he shouted. "Why shouldn't I? Who would care?"

I don't know what possessed me. I think I knew what he meant but I made myself sound cross and as ordinary as I could.

"Your mother would care," I said. "She'd have to clean up the mess. My mother says no man ever cleans up after himself."

He laughed — a croaky laugh, but it was a laugh.

"Oh, does she? I've cleaned up plenty of messes," he got out. "I hope you never see such bloody messes . . . "

I picked up the knife and dropped it into my coat pocket. I had no idea what to say next but I grabbed at the first idea that came and blurted it out. "If you hurt yourself, it would break your father's heart," I said. "And your mother's too."

He just stood there, holding onto the edge of the sink and shaking his head. He looked a bit dizzy.

So I reminded him that Dr. Webb went all the way to England to fetch him home. "Cornelia says he cries over you," I ended up.

"*He* never cries," he said. "None of the old men cry. They don't know how! Go away."

I had been backing toward the door. I knew he had seen where I put the knife. I forgot all kitchens have more than one knife and I wanted to escape before he tried to get it away from me. I made it out the back door and ran for home. Just as I got safely into our kitchen I remembered the meat on the floor. It would spoil if it was left. And Richard would not know what it was.

I didn't want to, but I made myself go back, and it still lay there. I heard Richard in the front of the house. He was singing in this sort of crazy voice. I didn't wait to hear more than a few words, and it wasn't until I was safe in my room that I knew he was singing, "Nine men slept in a boarding house bed." It is a silly song Hugo used to sing. I couldn't believe it. Why on earth would he be going to hurt himself one minute and start singing the next? I wonder what I ought to do with their knife.

❀

Saturday, March 10

I took the knife back in the same coat pocket. Mrs. Webb let me in. I stood there like a stick until she offered to get me a gingerbread man. When I nodded, she went to get it from the pantry. I slipped the knife into the sink, took the cookie, thanked her and left without ever saying a word about why I had come. She must have wondered. The gingerbread man was hard as rock. He must have been left over from Christmas. I gave him to Charlie, who will eat anything and hardly ever gets any sweet treats. While I was there, I could hear Richard and his father arguing in the front parlour. I was so glad to get away without meeting him.

Sunday, March 11

I can tell the war news is bad. Father hardly ever teases these days. We don't know where Hugo is right now. The Allies seem to be losing, but Hugo said in his last letter, "Never lose hope, Eliza. We will win. And I will see you again." I cling to that.

When I get to crying, Mother says, "Do not be tempted into the slough of despond, my daughter. Spring begins this month."

It does not look like spring but I will do my best not to despair.

Wednesday, March 14

It will soon be Easter but Moppy says she cannot make decent hot cross buns with sugar so dear and with the awful flour we get these days. Also we're supposed to be thrifty and not waste any food, but Mother will dye some eggs for the little ones. She has done without to save them up.

Yet I saw through Mrs. Burns's windows one day and there she sat gobbling down a big plateful of eggs and bacon. Her brother brings them from the farm. She never shares with anyone. Belle was sick and we needed special food for her and prices just seem to keep going up and up. And all the time Mrs. Burns seems to have everything she needs.

St. Patrick's Day

Saturday, March 17

Top o' the mornin' to you, dear Reader.

I have moved my journal upstairs. I kept missing out days with it in the basement. I am tired of running up and down to tell you things. I will leave you in my ribbon drawer today and tonight I will carry the trunk to our room and tell Verity what is in it and hang the key around my neck where she cannot get it.

As I wrote that, I realized that the two of us get

along better than we used to. I wonder why. Maybe it is having our brothers so far away. We have needed each other as friends in a way we didn't before. But I will hide my key anyway.

Tomorrow is the Missionary Society concert. I am reciting "Crossing the Bar" by Tennyson. It is sad but it sounds lovely. Like music.

Mother is making over a blouse which used to be hers. It is Chinese silk that Uncle Jack brought back from one of his sea voyages. I will wear it tomorrow night and on Easter Sunday with my plaid skirt and black velvet jacket. I am to have a new hat too. I was not going to, but Belle found my old one with the little nosegay on it and took it apart to make a wedding bouquet for her dolls. How clever of Belle!

Sunday, March 18

The concert was a great success. I brought tears to several eyes. I didn't hear sobs but they told me about the tears. Verity did very well too. Mother and I talked her out of rolling her eyes. We made more than two hundred dollars.

April Fool's Day

I caught a cold. Nothing as bad as Cornelia's grippe but I was sick enough not to feel like writing even to my dear Reader. But I am back again now and I will soon be right as rain.

Why do they say that? You would think it would be "right as sun."

Friday, April 6

The Americans have come into the war on our side at last! Surely their coming will turn the tide. Even Father looks more hopeful tonight.

Richard Webb had a relapse but seems to be improving again. I never go over there now. I have not seen him since the day I took the knife.

Everyone is singing American songs and nobody is saying that it took them a long time to see where their duty lay.

Easter Sunday
April 8

War news seems bad in spite of the Yanks. And spring is cold but we sang Jesus Christ Is Risen Today! and the old words rang out bravely just as they have every other year. Mother used onion skins and watercolour paints and did make lovely eggs for the three little ones. They were so excited. I tried to be glad I was not a little one any longer, but it was not easy.

Then, under the edge of the tablecloth, Mother

slipped me an egg which was a deep yellow with my name painted onto it in curly dark red letters. I turned it over slowly, marvelling. On the other side, it said *Daughter.*

"Not a changeling," she murmured.

I could not eat it. It is so beautiful and it gives me a warm feeling right down inside. It is sitting in the drawer with my penny whistle. I told Mother and she said it will go bad and I would have to eat it eventually or throw it away, and it wasn't a good idea to waste an egg.

"It's the memory you keep," she told me.

Easter Monday

Mother and Moppy have started spring cleaning. I have to dust the books. We own millions of books. Usually I am glad, but not at spring cleaning time. Dusting is easier than some jobs, though. Verity has been out beating rugs in the snow. Her hands were a purplish blue when she came in.

Tuesday, April 10

There was a great battle on Easter Monday. At Vimy Ridge. They said it could not be taken. The French were driven back and so were the British. But our Canadian boys took it! Father says they must have been planning it for weeks. It was a great victory! But many men died, I think.

It is hard to keep all the battlegrounds straight and they have such foreign names. I hope nobody we know was there. People go on and on about what a triumph it was for Canada, but we don't know the details yet. Perhaps, when it is in the paper, Father will let me cut it out and paste it in here. A victory, at last, after so many setbacks and defeats!

Verity and True went and got their hair bobbed in celebration. They look so changed. Verity does not look nearly so proper. She was actually dancing in our bedroom. I wonder what Grandmother will say. She said girls with bobbed hair were "fast" and "asking for trouble." I wonder what trouble she means.

I heard Verity humming tonight while she was taking her bath. "If you were the only boy in the world . . . " she sang.

I popped my head around the screen and asked her, "If who was the only boy?"

"Eliza Mary Bates, get *out!*" she shouted in a whisper. (It is perfectly possible to shout in a whisper.)

Susannah heard her too and we ran into Mother and Father's room and laughed until we cried. My stomach still hurts. I wonder what the boys will say when they come home and see her. I would not tell her this, but she looks prettier with short hair, almost dashing, like Lillian Gish.

Later

Father was not in the same mood as the rest of us. "Paid for with blood," was all he would say about Vimy Ridge. It is true that all the reports lately have been full of news about casualties, even as they praise the Canadians for taking the ridge. (They call one part of it the Pimple. Isn't that strange, dear Reader?)

Wednesday, April 18

Hugo was at Vimy Ridge and he is missing. The telegram came today. We must still hope. Everyone is celebrating the victory at Vimy, but not in our house.

But I am sure he will be found. He must be lying in a hospital with a wound and he has just lost his memory or something. I got up in the middle of the night last night and knelt down to pray and Verity woke up.

"Eliza, what is it?" she said.

I did not answer and then she slipped out from under the covers and knelt too, and we both prayed that our brother would be found. We did not say anything out loud but when we got back into bed, we both cried and cried.

God must listen. He *must.* If only Hugo is all right, I will be good forever and ever.

Thursday, April 19

Mother let me stay home from school today. It was a terrible day. I kept watching for a telegram. Nobody came. No news. She says I must go back in the morning because this may go on for months. It was as though the sun was stuck and the world could not move on.

Months! How could we bear it?

Friday, April 20

Mother sent me back to school. Her voice is steady but her lips are pale. It seems so strange. The little ones don't know what is wrong, but they know there is something. You can tell because they tiptoe and whisper and look afraid. Belle cries more than usual and cannot say what is the matter. Isaac wags his tail less and gazes up at us with big anxious eyes.

You would think pets would be in the way now, but it isn't true. Isaac and Ezekiel help us because they need to be cared for and they expect us to keep being our normal selves. Only it breaks all our hearts when Ezekiel speaks in Hugo's voice. I can't write for crying. But I am still hoping against hope that there is some mistake. In books, often in the last chapter, the soldier everyone thought was dead returns. But that is something that maybe only happens in stories.

At moments like this, dear Reader, it is hard to believe in you. And I cannot love God, even though I keep praying that He will find Hugo alive and whole. I don't want my brother to suffer.

But what about all the others? Who prays for them? And how does God decide?

I asked Mother. She says she thinks God does not decide the way I imagine. She says that wars are made by humans and humans must abide the consequences. "Pray for courage," she told me. "And faith and a loving heart."

"And for Hugo," I said.

She nodded. She could not speak and I saw her eyes were flooding.

Saturday, April 21

There is no use hoping. Our hope is gone, dear Reader. My brother is dead.

Mother and Father never say things like "passed away" or "gone to God" like other people do. They say the real word in a quiet, serious voice. I will try to do this too. But I understand why people use the other words. They are hiding from the terror of it.

Oh, how can I go on?

I stop writing and then I feel as though I am drowning.

I went to Mother and Verity came too and we all cried. But then somebody came. Moppy can only keep them off for so long. Everybody needs some-one to grieve with, Verity says.

But it will soon be time to go to bed. Will we sleep?

I will try to tell you how it happened. When the telegram came, it was late afternoon and we were all home. The Twins raced to get the door and then just stood there, so I went to let whoever it was in. It was Matthew Blake, who is one year ahead of me in school. He is at the high school and I won't be there until September. He stood there looking sick. I took the envelope and carried it in, leaving the door open.

"Shut the door, Eliza, for heaven's sake," Mother said. "We can't afford to heat all outdoors, not with this wretched stuff they call coal."

It is queer how clearly I can still hear what she said and how impatient she sounded.

Then she saw what I was holding. She held out her hand for it and I saw that her hand did not even shake though her face went wooden. She carried it straight to Father and I turned and went back to speak to Matthew. I had left him outside on the step without a word.

"Thank you," I said to him. Why did I thank him?

I kept hoping it was going to say Hugo was found, but it did not.

KILLED IN ACTION it said.

Father went white as marble.

These were the words, at least some of them.

DEEPLY REGRET TO INFORM YOU PTE
HUGO JAMES BATES INFANTRY OFFICIALLY
REPORTED KILLED IN ACTION.

We all hugged each other.

Father went to his Session meeting after Matthew left. There was some quarrel among two or three Elders and he said it had to be settled. Mother wanted to be with him but, of course, there are no women Elders and they would have known something was wrong. I don't see how he can face their eyes. I wonder if he has told them yet.

Later on

Mother just came in and found me lying wide awake with Verity sleeping next to me. She told me that Father was home and that he did not tell them about Hugo until after the meeting ended. They said his strength was an inspiration. Nobody dared to say anything about his sympathy for the German soldiers and how did he feel now knowing some Hun had shot Hugo. But a few probably thought such cruel thoughts. I just feel rage so boiling hot I can't bear it. I ache all over.

Sunday, April 22

Everyone feels so sorry for Mother and Father and so do I. But it is hard for everyone — even Belle, who still does not understand that Hugo is gone forever.

Cornelia came over with a loaf of fresh bread. "I'm sorry, Eliza," she said, looking at her feet. Then she kissed my cheek and ran for home. It was a wet kiss, which I was ashamed of myself for noticing. After all, it was sincere, and I cried after she was gone, the kind of crying that helps ease the pain.

I feel closer to Cornelia now, although I want Hugo back no matter what. Even as sick as poor Richard, even with a leg missing. He is . . . was strong and brave and I need him. It is hard to put this clearly, but the person I ache to talk to about all of this is Hugo himself. He is the one who would help me most when I feel as though inside of me there is no Eliza. There is only

I can't. I can't go on.

Wednesday, April 25

I have not been able to write, dear Reader. I could not think what to say. I would get out the journal and put it back without opening the cover. It felt as though I were frozen, or as if I were a girl made of *papier mâché*, which looks fine on the outside but is hollow inside, completely empty. I could move around but I was not me any longer. I was only a husk, like the coconut shell someone brought to us years ago after she'd been on a sea voyage.

Thursday, April 26

Belle found one snowdrop this morning in the corner of the garden where the house protects the earth. She brought it to me.

"Give it to Mother, Eliza," she whispered. We stared at its drooping head and remembered Hugo always gathering little bouquets for Mother early in the spring. I took her hand and we went together.

Mother gathered Belle onto her lap and they just sat and rocked for the longest time.

I found a tiny vase for the snowdrop and then Susannah marched out and, after quite a while, brought in two more. But spring has not come really, not here. Some day maybe. Not this year.

Friday, April 27

It is so strange. Being a minister's daughter, I am used to being with people who have had someone die. I have taken food to families who were grieving. I've visited homes filled with flowers. But nobody knows quite what to do when the lost person has died far away. For the first time, I understood why some people send flowers or food or notes with children and do not come themselves. They are afraid of saying the wrong thing.

I respect the ones who take the chance. The queerest thing is you often end up laughing. The ones I hate are the ones who hardly knew Hugo but come rushing over and sit and sit, with their eyes prying at your face, wanting to know what you are feeling behind your calm. They start sobbing on the doorstep and they always want to know every detail no matter how gruesome.

"Ghoul," Mother muttered when one of those went boo-hooing out the door.

People who have really suffered themselves are usually the kindest and they don't stay all day either. They come bravely to the door and they stay to talk a while.

The dreadful ones are forever pressing their hand on your head or grabbing you and squashing your face against their fronts. I can't say this to anyone but you, dear Reader, but I hate them all. Hugo would hate them too. They hurt Mother.

Charlie takes off the minute he hears a buggy pulling up or a car stopping. And Susannah runs after him. Deserters!

They ask if we are getting "our blacks" soon.

Mother manages to speak calmly, although I don't know how.

"Hugo hated black," she says and leaves it at that.

"An arm band would show you are grieving," one lady pressed.

Mother just looked at her and she went red and got up to go home.

Verity is being a tower of strength, as you would expect. I keep noticing little funny things Belle says or Isaac does, and tell Mother and Father to make them smile.

"You are a godsend, Eliza Mary," Father said and blew his nose very hard.

I wish Jack would come home. He just might. Compassionate leave, they call it. But Father thinks Jack will stay where he is — they need the pilots too much over there to send anyone home.

Saturday, April 28

I cannot bear it. I caught myself laughing out loud at Isaac today. How could I? Isaac had found a ball of knitting wool and started chasing it and it kept rolling away. He would growl at it and jump on it and shake it. Then, sure he had killed it, he would drop it and watch. It would begin to roll again and he would chase it once more, butting it with his nose. Finally he got to the top of the stairs and the yarn went bouncing over the top with Isaac staring after it. Then he flung himself down the steps and got his paws caught in it and went head over tail to the bottom. I was laughing already and then he stood up, sneezed, shook himself and stalked away, leaving the tangle of yarn behind. I laughed right out loud and then I remembered.

Father is shut in his room. Hugo is gone forever. Mother looks so worn and weary and brave. And I laughed at the dog! But you have to laugh. And, when I stopped, my cheeks were wet with tears.

Monday, April 30

We got through the last few days thinking nothing could be worse. But this morning a letter came from one of Hugo's friends. His name is David Martin. I don't know if I can write about it, but I feel as though I will break in pieces if I don't tell someone. Oh, dear Reader, I wish you were here to comfort me. I keep crying. Mother says tears only make your nose get stuffed up but I

Half an hour later

I had to stop but now I will go on. David Martin is in a hospital in France and he wrote a letter telling us the truth he was sure nobody else would tell us.

I was there on Easter Monday and I saw what

happened to Hugo. He was a great friend to me. I wish I had died and he had lived. I just got a Blighty, as we used to wish we would. They are sending me back to England because my foot was more or less shot off.

He went on to say that a nurse was coming back to Canada because of illness and he asked her to bring his letter out past the censors and mail it once she got home.

Then he told us the bad part.

Hugo did die at Vimy, but not because he was shot by the enemy. I still cannot take it in. But the letter said he had gone to help get a wounded man out of the line of fire. The soldiers had been ordered not to turn back no matter what. But the wounded man was a father with a new baby. When Hugo went to help him, a Canadian officer shot Hugo and killed him.

Captain Martin said that it could have been a mistake. It was dark. But he may have done it because Hugo disobeyed his orders.

Nobody really knows. Hugo's friend saw it happen. The next minute, the man who shot my brother was killed himself.

So Hugo, my Hugo, was shot down by one of our own troops.

Father burst out with a terrible groan. I had no idea what was wrong. I only learned the truth after I found the letter left on the table later on. I kept it and gave it to Mother so that Charlie would not come upon it. She said that was right. She said that telling people the truth would help nobody and Hugo would not want us to talk about it. I think I cannot bear it, but you can't stop bearing terrible things. They just go on being there. It is like being lost in the dark.

When I was nine I stayed out playing in the woods near Aunt Martha's until it got dark and I could not find my way out of the bushes and tree trunks. Hugo found me.

If only I could go into the dark and find him!

Jack might not even know yet. Perhaps he could not be reached at once.

Dear Reader, do you know what "a Blighty" is? It is something wrong with you that is bad enough to get you a leave in England. They are always making jokes about wishing for a Blighty.

Tuesday, May 1

Father did not get up this morning. He is not speaking to anyone, even Mother. The house is locked in a terrible stillness. Oh, dear Reader, I wish you were real and could come for a walk with me.

I want to go out into the country and climb a big hill and lie down in the long grass on the top and watch the clouds sail over me so peacefully. Hugo told me once to remember that those fat white clouds looked the same in Roman Britain. Shakespeare saw them looking exactly like that too. I must stop. It seems wicked to want to be peaceful when Hugo can't look up with me and share the peace.

Today four letters came from him, and one of them was just to me. I so wanted such a letter. I have not been able to read it yet. I cannot get past, "Dearest Monkeyshines." My hands start shaking when I see his writing. I have put it away and I will read it, but not yet.

When I opened the drawer, there was the penny whistle. I snatched it up, took it outside and threw it as far as I could. I threw it toward Cornelia's. I could not bear to keep it. Then, an hour later, I knew I had to get it back, but somebody must have come by, seen it on the ground and taken it. I searched and searched. Oh, Hugo, I will never be Monkeyshines again.

Thursday, May 3

Nothing gets any easier. And when it does, for a few minutes, I feel like a traitor to Hugo's memory.

Cornelia is restful. She does not expect much. I heard her telling Bertha that I was her best friend. I felt like saying it was not true. But perhaps it is.

She is making me a cross-stitch picture to hang in my bedroom. She won't let me see it until it is finished. I hope it is not religious. I've seen some she has done of children kneeling down saying prayers. They are revolting. Well, maybe I should not say so. But I would not want to have to sleep in the same room, and neither would Verity.

Very early, Saturday, May 5

I had a terrible dream. Everyone is still asleep except for me. Usually I would have Verity to turn to but Belle wanted Verity to come in with her in the night and I suppose she fell asleep there. The birds are singing madly but they can't make the horror go away.

I must write the dream down or I might slide back into it. I was on a big grey hill. I was in some dark and stony place. I was lost. Then suddenly I saw Hugo coming toward me. I tried to run to meet him. But my feet would not move. And then, just before he reached me, I saw it was not Hugo at all. It was a man like my brother but with no face. He fell to the ground and was swallowed up somehow and I saw another Hugo coming again from further back. And I tried to reach *him*. And it was another man with no face. Not even eyes. I think I am glad about the eyes. And I heard a moaning sound. I thought I would turn and run but I could not. And I saw the endless row of soldiers went on and on and then I woke up. I am still shaking. I have never had such a terrible nightmare. And who can I tell? I might tell Jack if he was home.

He cabled and has written, but it was just as Father thought. He is needed there because he is a trained pilot and they do not have enough. I wish the birds would stop. I am afraid to go back to sleep.

Oh, dear Reader, I do feel you listen. Writing it down makes it grow fainter. I am going to get up and go outside. The sun is up and the morning looks so lovely. I might get my letter from Hugo out now and read it. That would make the nightmare man — who wasn't Hugo at all but some monster — vanish, and my own brother come back to me.

That afternoon

As soon as I saw "Dearest Monkeyshines" I felt as though he had been given back to me. The letter told me more about Scrounger the cat and wished me luck on my exams and told me I should read a book called *A Little Princess.*

I read it long ago and loved it. I am glad it was such an ordinary letter. It was like having him come by for a visit. It made me cry buckets, of course, but that didn't matter.

Victoria Day,
May 24

This is supposed to be the day when you plant things in the garden. But we had hurricane winds and spurts of wet *snow!* Beastly weather. Spring only brought those few snowdrops and departed. There is a drought. Potatoes cost $4.00 a bag. Moppy says she can remember, a year or two ago, when the whole bag would not have cost more than a quarter.

What does the price of potatoes matter when there is no Hugo in the world?

Maybe spring will not come again. I know I wrote that before, dear Reader, but it is still how I am feeling. People with no brother to remember keep speaking of Vimy Ridge as though it were a great victory. The words sound like tolling bells to me. I can hear them over and over. I try not to think about it. But they keep telling how the soldiers swarmed up the ridge at dawn with the shells firing down on them. They don't tell about the thousands of soldiers who died taking that ridge, though, or the thousands of families who are mourning a loved one.

I can't stand it. I can't. And the grown-ups are all worried about Mother and Father as though Hugo meant nothing to the rest of us. I think some of them actually think we are too young to know what happened. Even Belle knows now, although not about the man who shot him being a Canadian.

Friday, June 1

Today is Verity's birthday. She is eighteen!

"At last!" she said at breakfast. Now what did she mean by that? She has changed lately. She just sits and stares into space and thinks and thinks about something. But when you offer her a penny for her thoughts, she just says her thoughts are worth much more than that.

Sunday, June 3

Father did not preach this morning. He has broken down under the nervous strain. That is what Mother says. Maybe it is something like what happened to Richard. Father cries and hardly ever comes out of his study. The church is giving him "leave of absence." I can hardly remember a Sunday morning in my life when my father did not give the sermon. We all actually stayed home. Reverend Archibald preached and he came to the house after the service, but he only stayed a few minutes. He went in to talk to Father and came out shaking his head.

"How was he?" Mother asked, her eyes filled with worry.

"He would not talk to me," Mr. Archibald said.

"We must give him time, Mrs. Bates. And pray for him, of course."

Monday, June 4

I got a letter from Jack! It is very short so I will copy it here.

Dear Eliza,

I keep thinking how lonely you must be. Hugo was your special brother and you were special to him too. Our family is not good at saying these things, but I miss him too and if I can help you somehow, write to me.

Love, Jack

His letter brought tears to my eyes but they did not hurt like other tears. It made me feel as though he had given me a big hug.

I picked up the mail this morning so nobody saw the letter come. I will show them later maybe. Right now it is private. I have not written back to him but I will.

Wednesday, June 6

Dear Reader, life seems never to be ordinary now. Mother came into Verity's and my room tonight and told me that she is sending the Twins and Belle and me away to Aunt Martha for a holiday. Father needs complete rest. Verity does not have to go because of her schooling, and because she works at the Red Cross now. She spends all her time over there, serving mugs of tea to other women rolling bandages or rolling them herself or packing boxes to be sent overseas. I wonder sometimes how the men feel when they find a toothbrush inside and soap and so on. I think they really want warm socks and Russian toffee much more. I stuck a copy of one of Hugo's books into a box going to him once and he wrote back as pleased as though I had sent him jewels.

I was stunned at the idea of leaving home but I managed to ask about *my* schooling. After all, I'm supposed to take the entrance exams that tell if you are ready to enter high school. But Mother said she had talked to my teacher and the principal and they are going to pass me without my writing the examinations. They said I was "a fine student with a good mind." I should be happy to hear that but it does not sound real, and it does not matter one whit.

How can I bear to be sent away? I cannot. I thought of refusing, but Mother looks so white and her eyes have grown huge and when she looks at me she reminds me of a wounded deer I saw once. Father took me on a walk in the woods with him. All at once a doe plunged out of the trees and passed us, not even noticing we were there. She had been shot in the flank but not killed outright. It was terrible.

She was so piteous. Hunters came crashing through the trees looking for her and Father pulled me away. We heard them shoot her and Father said it was good because she would not have to suffer any longer. But I still see her eyes in my dreams sometimes. I did not tell the younger ones.

"I know you want to stay, Eliza," Mother said in the new husky voice which is all we hear now. "But Aunt Martha will need you. Four children means a lot more work." She is right. There will be more food to cook, more clothes to wash and mend, more faces to scrub, more buttons to do up, lots more worry. "Also, whether you believe it or not," Mother finished up, "the younger kiddies will depend on you to comfort them. You will be their 'home' in a strange place. Father and I are counting on you."

There was nothing I could say after that so I nodded and managed not to burst into tears until I got to my own room. I've always wanted her to say words like those: "Father and I are counting on you." But hearing her say them in reality was not one bit the way I imagined. I wanted to feel important, but I just feel shut out and sent away. We go on the Monday train.

I remember longing to go out and lie on a grassy hill and stare up at the sky. Well, I will be able to at Aunt Martha's. I don't want to now.

Charlie wants to take Isaac with us but Aunt

Martha has her dogs and Mother told Charlie that Father needed Isaac to help heal his hurt. Charlie cried. When Mother tried to remind him how he had always loved Fleet and Scalawag, Aunt Martha's dogs, he roared out that he was *not* crying about leaving Isaac. He was crying because he wanted Hugo back. "Boys feel bad too," he gulped out and he sobbed against Mother's front.

That started Susannah sniffling and then Belle began to sob. I forced myself not to join in or the kitchen would have been under water. It is not only diphtheria and typhoid that are catching, but tears and laughter too. Giggles are more contagious than measles.

I helped mop up the flood. Yet all the time we feel so terrible, I smell the lilacs outside my window. They are so sweet you drink in their fragrance in great gulps. We had such a cold spring that I thought there would be no flowers. Snow in May! Then Belle brought in some small dandelions. They smell like dandelions even though they are only half grown. Hugo will never smell them again. Never again.

Later

I wrote to Jack and told him we are going to Aunt Martha's in Guelph. I said I copied his letter into my journal. I told him that, even though Hugo was special, I loved him too and we all miss him. That was all I could manage.

Sunday, June 10

We went to church this morning without Father. Mother kept us at home until the last minute so nobody had a chance to cry over us, I think. She did not say so but I am pretty sure I am right. I noticed we all kept our eyes on *The Book of Praise* instead of looking around as usual. When it was over she led us out the side door and home at a gallop. Nobody mentioned anything except Charlie, who said that if we'd been in a race, we'd have won hands down.

Monday, June 11

I am writing this on the train. It makes my pen jiggle. The Twins are across the aisle reading and watching out the window. Belle is asleep against me but my writing does not seem to trouble her. Her eyelids are still puffy from crying when Mother stood waving to us. Belle has never gone anywhere without Mother before. I have not gone away from her very often either. Mother's eyelids were red, although she did manage not to break down at the station. Father was at home and acted as though we were not leaving.

We spent last night packing. It was strange. I kept feeling little shooting bits of excitement because we were going on a trip and we might have a grand time. Part of me could hardly wait until I was sitting on the train smelling that sooty train smell and hearing the whistle and chugging out of the station. And another part felt shoved out of the nest and forsaken. The moment came when Mother and Verity said goodbye to us. At the last minute, even Charlie was rubbing away tears. Once we got out of the station we opened the lunch Moppy had packed for us, and which we were supposed to save until noon. She had made us lovely devilled eggs. We jammed them into our mouths and gulped them down whole. We crammed in the bread and butter too and we had food smeared all over our lips and chins. We did stop at last and left a bit for later. But somehow eating that way helped us stop feeling so totally empty and pushed aside. It is as though, now there is trouble at home, we aren't wanted. Being bad comforted us, and I am glad we did it even though I should feel sorry for misbehaving. I am supposed to be a Good Example. Mother should not expect it of me. Verity is the one who's been practising that part ever since she was a baby.

"You know what?" Belle said all at once in a cozy little voice. "We are being sent into exile like a prince in a story."

We all laughed at her, especially because she made it sound fine and dandy. But it helped me, thinking I was like some poor princess sent away by her cruel uncle into the wilderness.

"I think we are like Heidi," Susannah said. "But we do have each other."

Aunt Martha's is not like Klara's house in Frankfurt, but it is good to pretend. We still have a long way to go. We have to change at Union Station. Mother said they could get someone to help us but I have done it before. We will be fine. All the same, I'll be glad when we're on the train to Guelph.

In the next train

We made the switch without a hitch. Charlie was a great help. He keeps calm.

Belle has gone back to sleep, which is a blessing. People keep getting on and off. Here comes a soldier in uniform.

I cannot concentrate any longer, dear Reader. Excuse me.

Bedtime, at Aunt Martha's

Just after I stopped writing, Belle woke up and brought up her boots. She got vomit all over both of us. Thank goodness she missed the journal! (I am devoted to you, dear Reader, but I don't think I could have gone on writing in a book covered with puke.) Did you know that Shakespeare describes babies as "mewling and puking in their nurse's arms." Isn't that revolting? When Father read that bit aloud to me he said, "No wonder the man spent most of his time writing plays away from home."

I was so mortified. We got most of the vomit off in the tiny, tilting bathroom, but she kept weeping and wanting to go home.

That soldier saved the day. He had one pant leg folded up and he walked with crutches. But he was funny, kind and he likes children. He began teasing right away and he made Belle laugh in spite of herself. When her head popped up over the seat Charlie told her to keep her head down, as if she were a soldier in a trench.

Then we all sang "It's a Long Way to Tipperary" and "Pack Up Your Troubles." Charlie asked the soldier what the men thought was the hardest thing to bear in the War. He was serious but the soldier made joking answers. "No dry socks," he said.

"No. I mean really," Charlie said.

"Oh, you mean really. Well, here's the real answer. Having no mother to tuck me in," he grinned.

Susannah hissed to Charlie that his wound was worst.

"No, no," the soldier said. "Losing that leg got me sent home." He told us he was being eaten alive by bugs of every kind imaginable, and drowned in mud in the trenches. Now, he said, still teasing, the minute he gets home, he'll get to sleep in his very own bed without being chewed on by things too terrible to mention. "And I won't have to worry about sausages falling on me any longer."

Belle stared at him goggle-eyed. "I love sausages," she said.

Charlie told her the soldier was teasing. Then the man himself told her the "sausages" he was talking about were bombs. We told him about Hugo and he said we should be very proud to have a brother who had served at Vimy Ridge.

"We are proud," Susannah said softly.

Then the soldier, whose name turned out to be Timothy Whitney, had to get off. And then we were at the station in Guelph.

Aunt Martha was there to meet us in her red velvet hat. She calls it her small rebellion hat. We came out here in their gig. The Twins squashed together and I held Belle perched on my lap. Aunt Martha kept telling Blueboy to hurry up and he ambled along at his usual clip-clop.

"He's a lovely horse," I said.

Brace yourself for a shock, dear Reader. Aunt Martha looked at me sideways and said she was getting a Tin Lizzie.

"You can't drive," yelled clever Charlie.

"I will be able to by the time I bring Lizzie home," said our shocking aunt. "I'm having lessons." I don't know whether it is true or a joke.

I have a room all to myself. It gives me the strangest feeling. I have shared with my sister ever since I moved out of a crib. Dear Reader, believe it or not, I miss Verity. And I need my penny whistle.

Friday, June 15

We all feel so far from home. This afternoon I took the younger children down to the river to swim. I reminded them how lovely it is to have the Speed River close by, so we can swim whenever we like. The mill pond in Uxbridge is not the same. What I said was true but we went right on being homesick.

"I'd rather not swim and get to stay home," Charlie grumbled.

The others all agreed, with faces as cheerful as tombstones. I was standing on the bank watching them paddle when Belle was pushed under by Susannah. I jumped in to rescue her and then I stopped being all prissy and nearly grown up. I became the Princess Wild Rose, and Belle was my baby sister. We were fleeing from Charlie, who was a wicked baron. Susannah named him "The Archduke Ferdinand." The real archduke got shot in Sarajevo in 1914 and that was what started the War, but not one of us knows exactly who he was. His name is just right for a villain. Susannah was his evil henchman, slinking about like the villains in Jo March's plays.

Belle stopped, all at once, and said, "Was the real archduke on our side or theirs?"

Nobody was clear about this detail.

"Do you mean that Hugo got killed all because of some archduke we don't even *know?"* my small sister pronounced. Her cheeks went very red and her eyes shot sparks.

"There was more to it," I said. "But you will have to ask Father to explain it. I can't."

It does sound crazy. But she gave up the subject, at last, and we went back to our game.

We got soaking wet. Belle screamed such deafening shrieks when she got kidnapped by brigands, that two women who live nearby came out on their front verandahs to see if she was in danger. She stood up, with river water running off her in streams and said, very sweetly, "I'm fine. I'm only a baby princess who is about to be carried off by that evil Archduke Ferdinand."

The taller lady looked surprised. Then she laughed. "What will he do to you?" she asked.

"Inflict some vile torture in his castle dungeon, I expect," said Belle cheerfully.

"Dear me," said the lady shaking her head. Then

she asked if we were the Bates children. We nodded and her face stopped smiling. "I was so sorry to hear about your loss," she told me.

Her eyes dug into me like fishhooks. I think she was waiting for me to cry. I grabbed Belle by her sopping wet shoulder and swung her around. When I growled at her to come along home she did not fuss. Neither did the other two.

"Old cat," Charlie muttered. Thank goodness his voice was low enough so I could pretend I had not heard him.

Then, as we sloshed along in shoes full of muddy water, Belle asked if I thought we were like the soldiers in the trenches.

I looked down at Belle, who was still waiting for me to answer. The mud on our shoes was nothing compared to what I had heard Richard Webb and others speak of. I started to tell her how awful it was and then stopped. It was like Hugo writing me a cheerful letter. She is so tender-hearted. So I just nodded.

Aunt Martha shook her head over us, but stayed calm. I suppose she is used to children getting dirty. There is more mud in the country. Guelph is not really the country, but Grandmother and Aunt Martha live by the river in the old farmhouse just beyond the edge of town. Grandfather farmed there until he died and now other farmers rent the land.

I think maybe Aunt Martha feels as sorry for us as that lady who talked to us at the river. But our aunt is not the kind of person who makes a big to-do over a bit of dirt.

She just got us to take off our shoes and then she handed me the floor mop. I was glad Moppy had brought me up to know how to get a muddy floor sparkling clean.

Saturday, June 16

Aunt Martha astonished me tonight. She really *is* having driving lessons so she can buy herself a car. I think she is the only woman driver I know personally.

"Eliza, you will soon have the vote. Do you want to be a modern woman or not?" she said.

I almost said that Verity does not want to drive or vote, but then I wondered if I was wrong about my big sister. She looks so different with her hair bobbed and she is acting differently too. Maybe she is turning into a modern woman. I certainly want to vote and drive.

Sunday, June 17

We went fishing this afternoon. It is lovely to be far enough away from home that Father's flock cannot see us and disapprove of what we do. We caught eleven fish. They were very small, but Aunt Martha and I cleaned them anyway and she fried them for our supper. I am not usually a girl who loves to eat fish, but I enjoyed those. Delectable and crisp as crispy. Aunt Martha used corn meal to fry them in, with wheat being scarce. But she also used lots of butter. They still have their little Jersey cow Lizabelle. She was born when Belle was a baby and got named after us. She is so gentle. Susannah and Charlie have both learned to milk her. Belle wants to but her hands are too small, I think.

"Let's stay until we catch one hundred next time," Charlie said, staring mournfully at the empty platter.

Monday, June 18

Today I missed Cornelia. I was surprised. Even though Susannah is smarter than Cornelia in some ways, Corny is nearer my age and she thinks about the same things. We wonder about growing up. Well, maybe Corny does not wonder when she is alone, but she listens while I talk about our bodies. She blushes. I think it is silly to blush because your body is changing. Since I have always shared a room with Verity, I know things Corny doesn't.

We went to Aunt Agnes's house today and ended up looking at photograph albums. We saw pictures of Mother and her two sisters when they were our age. I look like Aunt Martha, Verity looks like Aunt Agnes, Susannah looks like Mother and Belle looks like herself.

Grandmother told me I was the "spitting image" of Martha. I wonder why people say that. I asked her. She had no idea.

They also say Charlie is "a chip off the old block," meaning he looks like Father. Why are girls never chips off the old block? I guess it would be peculiar to think of your mother as an old block of wood. Yet wood can be beautiful.

I feel guilty enjoying the country food so much. We have real butter and an egg every day. Bacon too and pork sausages. We brought those home from Aunt Agnes's house. I wonder what Father would say about it when we're all supposed to be doing without.

I told Grandmother what I was thinking. Her answer shocked me but made me laugh too. "What the eye doesn't see, Eliza," she said with a little grin, "the heart doesn't grieve over."

When I wrote a letter home, I didn't tell about the food.

Wednesday, June 20

I want to go home in the worst way. Mother sent a letter to Aunt Martha and told her to tell me that

Cornelia is very ill. She got red measles and then complications of some kind. This can be very dangerous. They are worried about her heart. Mother said to pray for her. I am trying. But I don't know which are the right words. Mother says she is relieved Belle is far from the contagion.

Tuesday, June 26

Belle is ill too, but she does not have measles. She has a head cold. It wouldn't be bad if it weren't for her delicate health. Colds always go to her chest. Aunt Martha says there is nothing to worry about. Belle does look pitiful, though, and she begs for Mother to come. Mother wrote to say that as soon as Belle is well enough, we can all come home. Thank goodness! I didn't ask, but Father must have recovered his strength.

Mother did not say a word about Cornelia's health. I hope she is getting better. Surely she must be. She can't be contagious any longer or Mother would not let us come near.

Tuesday, July 3

At last, a letter came from Jack and it was to *me*. He got my letter telling him we were going to Guelph. He wants me to go and visit Norah, his old sweetheart, and tell her that he has fallen in love with someone in England, and he is sorry but he does not want her to build up false hopes.

How could he have done it in such a short time? Well, I suppose six months is time enough.

I don't see how I can do it. I let Aunt Martha read the letter, even though he asked me not to tell Father and Mother. He does not want to worry them.

Aunt M. sighed and gave me a strange look. Then she said I must go. She will drive me over there to-morrow and I can walk home.

The girl's name is Rosemary and she is a nurse. He and Rufus met her at a hospital in England when they were visiting a fellow pilot who had been injured.

Wednesday, July 4

I did it. Aunt Martha drove me in the buggy to Norah's today. I told her that Jack was in love with an English girl. That was what he asked me to say.

She looked as though I had stabbed her in the back. Her eyes scared me, dear Reader. She is always pale, but she looked as though she might swoon like some girl in a romance novel. Then she cried without making a sound. I went to put my arms around her but she stiffened like an ironing board and backed away. At last, she spoke in a thin hard voice.

"I suppose he has found someone prettier," she

said. "Trust Jack to pick up a sweet little English floozie instead of keeping his word to me."

I just looked at her. I do not know what Rosemary looks like, but there are not many girls prettier than Norah. I almost told her so because I did feel sorry for her, but Jack said, in his letter, that he was glad now that Norah had insisted they make no promises to each other about the future. She had told him that they must stay free. And I wondered, all at once, why. Had she wanted *him* to be free, or herself?

It was a horrible moment, dear Reader. I was sorry for her, but I was angry deep inside to hear her lie about my brother Jack, who is the soul of honour.

"You had better go home, Eliza," she said. She didn't offer me a cool drink. She didn't even walk me to the door. But I could see she was going to really start crying as soon as I shut it behind me. Maybe I should have tried to hug her but I could not do it. She had put up a wall.

I was halfway home and crying myself sick when along came Aunt Martha and Blueboy to pick me up after all. "Was it very hard?" she asked. I nodded.

"Well, Eliza my dear, don't break your heart over Lady Norah," she said. Then she told me that Norah has not missed a party since Jack left, and is going out steadily with the Burrows boy. I remember him. He has poor eyesight. "Norah will not stay on the shelf grieving, you may be sure," Aunt Martha finished as we arrived home. I got out of the buggy and, although it was so hot, I felt cold inside as well as sad, and somehow ashamed. But not of Jack. I think Jack is almost noble.

Friday, July 6

We go home tomorrow morning. Aunt Martha is coming with us to help while Moppy goes for her visit to her sister's. A neighbour girl will stay here with Grandmother. Belle still is pale, but her eyes shine at the thought of being home with Mother.

They are not saying anything about Jack. I hope he has been writing to them. I feel guilty when I get a letter if they have had none.

Monday, July 9

We are back now. And Father is better, although quieter, and he looks older. He has stopped teasing too. He and Belle sit together and say not a word, just somehow take comfort from each other.

I actually found I was trying to stop thinking of Hugo's being dead. I wanted to stop hurting. I was furious with myself.

Thursday, July 12

It is Orangemen's Day and there's to be a parade. Father says he wants us to stay home. He says the parade is perpetuating hatred. He is hard to understand.

Mother says she has plenty of work for us to do tending the garden and starting preserving. I cannot believe it is really time for that, not after such a slow spring. I like eating what is in the jars, but preserving is such long hot work and it goes on forever.

Sunday, July 15

Father preached about the Prodigal Son this morning. Do you like him, dear Reader? I never have. I feel too sorry for the elder brother, although he does sound a little like Verity. Father says the story should not be called the Prodigal Son but the Forgiving Father. This morning I wondered, for the first time, what really made that father run. I don't think my father would run, but he is a dignified man. Maybe the bad son felt ashamed at the last minute and turned away. Then his father would have run. But the boy does not sound like someone who would feel ashamed.

Cornelia has recovered but she looks so different. She does not have a pudding face any more. She is pale as milk and has no strength. She reminds me of a stalk of celery that has been left in water too long, all limp and bendy. Dr. Webb is talking of moving away from Uxbridge.

Guess what, dear Reader? This will astonish you. I truly hope she does not go. She is not a kindred spirit, but we are friends.

No letters have come from Jack to Mother or Father for nearly three weeks. Nobody says anything. Verity seems to get all the mail these days and she is secretive about it. The envelopes are big and official looking. I wonder what she is up to.

I miss being in the country. I wanted to come home so much, but it is a bit tame here. We still have war work, of course. Bandages to roll, boxes to pack and soldiers to write to. I am glad I don't have to write to strangers the way some girls do. I write to Jack. We also go out collecting bits of scrap metal for the war effort. We also weed the stupid garden. Everyone was too busy while we were gone so the plants are not all that healthy. The watermelon vines I planted are growing well though. It will be lovely to eat something so sweet and not have to stint.

Being at Aunt Martha's was a happy time in some ways. We went on walks in the woods most every day. Because Grandmother and Aunt Martha live close to the edge of town, we could walk down by the river or out to the ridge. I know there are birds and stars and trees and everything in Uxbridge but they seem closer and more our own private blessings at the farm. The moon is bigger and the stars are brighter and closer there without so many buildings close by. My room at Aunt Martha's had a high casement window and, when I lay in bed, one star shone in at me particularly brightly. I felt as though it knew I was there and I could talk to it about Hugo. It helped, somehow, that he must have seen it shining too, since he was always a stargazer. He taught me how to see the Big Dipper and Orion with his belt and Vega and Cassiopeia and so many more. The others weren't interested, so it was special between Hugo and me. When I was at Aunt Martha's, I taught Charlie and Susannah to find them and, when Belle can stay up late enough, I will teach her too.

I kept thinking that Hugo would never again see violets in the grass or the kingfisher down by the pond at Aunt Martha's or the sun on Belle's hair when it is just washed and looks like spun gold. Then, today, I made up my mind that it is up to me to see them all and enjoy them for him. I will try anyway. And, whenever I see something special, I will not only see it for Hugo, but remember him while I look. He would want me to be happy remembering him because we were always so happy when we were together.

Oh, that is fancy talk, but I want to feel his arms

hug me and hear his laughing voice say, "Hello, Monkeyshines!" I thought, at first, that I could not bear it, but you do not get to stop bearing it if you keep living. So I'll turn it around and try to make it into something good.

Wednesday, July 18

Dear Reader, another terrible battle in which many Allied soldiers died. We don't know much about it yet except it is happening at Passchendaele.

I really thought the War would be over by this time, especially now the "Yanks are in it," as the song says. "Over there, over there . . . "

Thursday, July 19

Dear Reader, I got another letter from Jack and it is astonishing. He and Rufus *both* love Rosemary. Jack finally told Rufus that he wanted to ask her to marry him, and Rufus said he thought as much, but *he* wanted to ask her himself. So — and this is the amazing part — they tossed a coin to see who would propose first. Jack won the toss. But Rosemary said she did not love him like that. She felt like a sister to him.

The next weekend they had leave, Rufus asked Rosemary to marry him and she said yes. They are not supposed to marry while they are at war, or something like that — I don't understand why not

— so they must wait. And Jack will be their best man.

He says he has to talk to someone about it or he might burst, and he is sorry if I don't want to hear all his news. He would have told Hugo, but Hugo is gone and he thinks Verity would not understand. I think he might be right.

I wrote back and told him I was honoured to be confided in and I thought Rosemary was crazy to like Rufus better. Rufus is nice but Jack is the prime article.

I do feel sorry for him. Rosemary is a nursing sister in a convalescent hospital near their aerodrome. She worked there before the War when it was a children's convalescent hospital and she stayed on. She is a civilian though, not an army nurse. For some reason, this makes things better for Rufus. Jack did not say why. Maybe she can leave the hospital without having to get permission from an officer. That is probably it.

Saturday, July 21

Jack sent me a picture, but Rosemary is standing between him and Rufus and is too small to show up clearly. They are in uniform and she has on her nurse's uniform with a strange, high cap.

"Hugo would understand how I feel," Jack said.

It is true. My brother Hugo was the most understanding person I have ever known. But the strange thing is that I believe I understand too. I have not been in a battle, but I have sat with Richard Webb. I didn't write about it but he and I have become friends in the past few days.

It was all because of talking about the trenches. He was sitting in their garden after dark, crying. I could hear him and he was going on about the black mud.

I went over because nobody else was paying attention. He had a letter from a friend at the Front. It told terrible things. So many are dying.

I cried too and now he and I are friends but I have not told anyone. They might make fun of us or of him. And Mother and Father might worry. They do worry about unnecessary things.

Jack and Rufus have been flying night after night. They are too busy and tired to write much. That is what he tells Mother and Father. I keep going to the post office to pick up the mail so they won't know when I hear from him and they do not.

"He is so busy," Mother says, sighing.

Too busy with Rosemary, I think, but I keep my mouth shut about that.

Mother looks happier. She does not laugh though, even when Charlie is cutting up a lark.

They clearly were comforted by the letter that came yesterday.

Tuesday, July 24

Isaac killed a baby rabbit this afternoon. I don't know if Belle will ever forgive him. He did not tear it apart, just shook it by the neck. It looked exactly like Peter Rabbit in our Beatrix Potter books. Isaac has killed a few rats and even Belle thought that was fine. Her face is swollen from weeping and every time she looks at the poor dog she says, "Murderer!" He hangs his head. I wonder if he will remember next time a little rabbit ventures into the vegetable garden.

Tuesday, July 31

They go on and on fighting at the Front. It sounds dreadful. Richard has nightmares. I told him about my dream after Hugo died. He just looked at me.

"It is bad," he said, "but worst of all are the ones which cannot be told and which come back again and again."

He shuddered and sweat came out on his face. I did not ask any questions. It might help him to talk but it would not help me to listen.

I did ask how long a battle could last.

"Weeks," he said in a dead cold voice that frightened me. When I looked at him, he seemed not to know me. I was so nervous, all at once, I jumped up and ran home.

Wednesday, August 1

Cornelia came running to our house this morning. Richard has had another nerve storm. He had to be hospitalized in the night. His father could not quiet him this time. I am such a coward. I was so glad she did not tell us about any of it until it was over. I am not much of a friend. Poor Richard.

I am sure it was hearing from his friend that upset him so.

Friday, August 3

Richard is going to be staying at a special hospital in Cobourg for some treatment. He frightens me sometimes, even though we are friends. Last time I looked into his eyes, it was as though he had gone away from himself and left only a husk behind. Some kids say their parents say "shell shock" just means you are a coward and lost your nerve, and that it is put on to get out of going back to the trenches. They have never looked into Richard's eyes or watched him when he breaks down.

The Webbs have invited me to go with them to their summer place in Muskoka for two weeks, to be company for Cornelia. The little ones thought I was the luckiest girl alive, but I do not want to go. Dr. Webb is always criticizing.

I thought I would have to go, and I know they are nice to ask me. I said I had to ask permission, but I know I will get it.

I told Mother last night just before I went up to bed. This morning she gave me a long look when we were by ourselves. She said she thought it would be kind of me to accept, for Cornelia's sake, but she could understand my reluctance. "Would you be happy to go for a weekend if you did not have to stay longer?" she asked.

I nodded. I was so relieved she did not ask me to explain. She said she would tell them she could only spare me for the weekend.

But I agreed, in the end, to go for a week. Cornelia cried and I gave in. I feel homesick already and I have not left yet. I don't like being away from home right now.

Cornelia is as happy as a baby with a feather duster. Have you ever seen a baby playing with feathers, dear Reader? Belle used to lie absolutely entranced with Mother's.

Windermere House, Muskoka
Tuesday, August 7

We are here at a fancy summer hotel. We came up on the train and were met at the station. The Webbs brought mountains of luggage. Some families come for the entire summer and a boat takes them to their cottages. Vegetables come by boat and newspapers and laundry and almost anything else you can imagine. People play tennis and croquet. We have been out for a ride on Lake Rosseau on the steamer. Tomorrow we are going to visit friends of the Webbs' in Port Carling and I will see the locks. I was the soul of politeness, dear Reader, and did not tell them I don't care about such things. Maybe it will be fascinating.

But I did find some old books here in the "library," which is a dim room with big chairs. Some of the books are new but lots have been left by previous guests. I just finished *Prudence of the Parsonage*. It is a bit goody-goody. Prudence won't let any boy kiss her because she is saving her first for her husband. It sounds nice but not very real.

Life at Windermere is very posh. You have to watch your manners. We dress up for supper as though it is Sunday. Nobody talks about the War, but I think that is only because everyone knows about Richard. I'm glad they don't know about

Hugo, although I am afraid Mrs. Webb will confide in them. One lady has patted me already, as though I am her puppy dog.

One of Dr. Webb's friends took us for a drive. I like going for car rides except for having to stop to change the tires. I should warn Aunt Martha about what a nuisance this is. But, on the other hand, Blue-boy leaves steaming droppings on the road behind.

Thursday, August 9

I should be longing to stay here but I am longing to go home instead. Tomorrow we are taking the train to Algonquin Park. Each day that passes I check off on my secret calendar.

Sunday, August 12

We went to a little church in Windermere today. I felt strange being at church without one of my family. Some of the summer visitors, especially the men, had trouble singing the hymns, even Holy, Holy, Holy. We sang All Things Bright and Beautiful and it seemed to be written about Muskoka, even though there are no purple-headed mountains here. There *are* huge rocks that give you a strong feeling of God though.

True is trying to teach me to play tennis. I hope I do learn because I could play with Jack when he comes home. He is a very good tennis player. Verity plays but she is too timid. I think True is bored too. Why didn't she ask Verity to come? I told her she should have and she smiled and said, "Your sister has other plans."

What on earth did she mean by that?

Monday, August 13

We went to Canoe Lake. I saw bears, raccoons, deer (one was a doe with a fawn), porcupines and a beaver swimming. We also saw lots of birds. A tiny deer ate right out of my hand, dear Reader. It was so wonderful. And we went for a canoe ride. I learned to paddle bow while kneeling on the dock, and then Dr. Webb took me out with him. Cornelia would not go, which was good. She gets too flustered. She could have tipped us over in one of her panics. I liked Dr. Webb when we were out on the lake. It was so tranquil that all my fear of him just dropped away. I wish, dear Reader, that you had been with us. He even began to sing while we paddled. He sang "The Skye Boat Song" and "The Road to the Isles."

Thursday, August 16

Home again, home again, jiggety jig.

We are home in Uxbridge at last.

Saturday, August 18

When we arrived home on Thursday I found I had three letters from Jack waiting for me. Mother handed them to me with a curious look. "I didn't know you had become Jack's confidante," she said.

She wanted to read the letters, but I asked if they had not heard from him too. They had. So I smiled and said he told me about the girls he was meeting in England.

She asked if I thought he was serious about any one of them.

"He likes Rufus's girl best," I said. I kept my voice light and she looked relieved. I did not say he only wrote to me so he would have somebody to talk to about Rosemary. But it is true. He goes on and on telling me how funny she is and how kind and how much Rufus loves her.

They might be married by now. Rufus asked his commanding officer for leave and he would not grant it to him. He disapproves of wartime marriages. He says that worrying about a wife interferes with a pilot's concentration. But Rufus is getting a special license, and another pilot, who is a minister in civilian life, will perform the ceremony. Jack says that if Rufus does not get permission, they will marry anyway and then do it with permission after the war is over.

Jack was still going to be the best man. He wrote

the letter back in early July. Letters take an age sometimes and then I was away when it arrived. Rufus had a leave coming up and they were planning to do it then. It is a dead secret. Rufus would be in big trouble if the news got out that they had married without leave.

In the third letter Jack said he had promised he would take care of Rosemary if anything should happen to Rufus. But nothing will, he said.

Reading the words made me shiver, though. He hardly mentions the flying they do or the dangers they face. But everyone knows how dangerous it is.

Tuesday, August 21

Here is a monumental news flash, dear Reader. Verity told me and the infants last night that she is not going to go to Normal School and train to be a teacher after all. She is going to be a nurse. She applied to the Sick Children's Hospital as soon as she turned eighteen. Mother and Father were worried, at first, that the work might be too hard for her. She said she was not going to the Crimea and that conditions had changed since Florence Nightingale's day.

Her Red Cross work persuaded her, and nursing Belle through her bilious attacks and fever. She was so calm and comforting and Belle clings to her. Hearing the veterans talk too was part of it.

Saturday, September 1

Verity has packed her things and moved out. Our bed feels enormous and, last night, how I wished I still had my penny whistle! Not to hear Verity breathing close to me is so eerie.

Monday, September 3

I neglected you, dear Reader, because I wrote to Jack and went to church and Sunday school and read a wonderful book called *The Harvester.* David Langston is the man I want to marry except, of course, Gene Stratton-Porter married him off to Ruth James. He practically *glows* with health and goodness and I love his dog and his cabin. I have put it on the shelf where I keep Read Again Soon books.

Jack has never said if R. and R.'s wedding took place. Maybe he is afraid someone would see the letter, but I keep them hidden away in a very safe place.

I have started high school and am in the First Form. It is different. There are so many more students and the noise they make is startling. I think I will get to like it. But I do feel shy. We will be doing some Shakespeare. That's exciting.

Wednesday, September 5

I got another letter from Jack. It is utterly different from the earlier ones. He says nothing about a wedding. I will copy out a bit of it but not all.

Eliza, sometimes I do get frightened. Yesterday our section got caught in a heavy fog and only three of us came safely home. One went down and we have no idea what happened to him — the fog was so thick. The fighting was heavy and we lost sight of him. We joke around and pretend we are invincible, but under the acting we are all afraid that next time we'll be the ones missing.

I think they may be transferring Rufus and myself into a program to train new pilots. We pretend it is a bore, but the relief is enormous. I am not a born fighter like Billy Bishop or the Red Baron. That sort seems most alive when they are airborne. This is not the case with Rufus or myself.

I should not go on like this, but we do go to visit some of our old friends who are now in the hospital where Rosemary nurses. I cannot tell you of them. I must stop this. It is not fair of me to talk this way to you when you are only twelve.

At that point, he signs off. But last night I could not sleep for worrying about him.

Thursday, September 13

Everyone in town is so excited to have some good news. The 116th made a raid near Coulott, in the Lens district, and they did so well that General Currie even mentioned them.

I am going to paste in what was in today's newspaper.

The battalion is the baby battalion of its corps, but it has reason to be proud of its record. It put on one of the finest raids that has ever been made in France, and owing to the gas attack having been launched when the battalion was getting into the assembly position, it would have been quite justifiable to have called off the raid, but by courage and determination they made it one of the most successful raids that has ever been made.

Monday, September 17

The War drags on and on. But Jack and Rufus are still all right and Jack has not written me another letter like that shocking one.

I like my English teacher. I memorized two poems for Memory Work, "Oh, to be in England now that April's there" by Robert Browning, and "How do I love thee? Let me count the ways" by Elizabeth Barrett Browning. All the other girls liked the love poem best and I liked it too, but I did like that "wise thrush" who "sang his song twice over lest you should think he never can recapture that first fine careless rapture."

The Twins are in disgrace because we had a missionary come to preach and, after dinner, when he was napping on the sofa right under the window, they tied a wet rag onto a stick and put it through the window and dropped it right into his open mouth. "He was snoring prodigiously," Belle said in their defense. He went red as a beet and left on the early train.

Father sat the Twins down for a lecture about what is due to a guest, but I could hear a quiver in his voice, so of course the Twins could too. Then Susannah burst out with, "He kicked Isaac. We all saw him."

"And he called him a misbegotten cur," Charlie said.

Father tried to go on with the lecture but he was angry at Mr. Buller himself. He said we must remember our manners in future even if a guest forgets his.

"And Father will never, ever invite him here again, will you, Father?" Belle chirped.

I wish Jack had been here to see Father's face. He could not decide whether to laugh or look like Moses scolding the Hebrew people.

Monday, October 8

Verity came home for a flying visit from Sick Kids. She was lucky to get the weekend off. She says she is gaunt with hunger and worn to skin and bone with working like a slavey. She is thinner, but she has a sparkle in her eyes. She tried to talk True Webb into training with her. But the minute the subject of bedpans came up True said no thank you.

Some nurses have gone over to the Front and come back with harrowing tales. Verity hears all about them even though she is working with children. She's always going on about famous nurses like Edith Cavell and Florence Nightingale.

She also tells us that she and the student nurses work such long hours to pay for their training and then they have to attend lectures and study. She has fallen asleep with her head on her book three times, and once she was so tired she did not wake up until morning. She had a stiff back all day and the matron told her to step along. "You'd think you were ninety," she snapped.

Verity laughs when she tells these stories. I've never seen her so happy. She made us more thankful, dear Reader. Listening to Father trying to tell us all to be thankful this morning, when so many people in the congregation were worried sick about their sons or husbands at the Front, was hard for everyone. But we all sang, O God, Our Help in Ages Past, with a will and it made me feel stronger somehow.

When Mother and Father had callers, Verity told the Twins and me the craziest story. She went into her room in the nurses' residence and put her hand into her dresser drawer looking for her camera. Instead of finding it, she found a whole nest filled with baby mice. Her friends had followed her in so she picked up one of these tiny mice and dangled it in front of them.

"Look what I've got," she said. The other girls shrieked and ran out. They took refuge in the room next door. She could tell they were all holding the door shut against her and her mouse. So Verity went to the window, climbed out on a ledge, side-stepped along it, got to the next room and put her foot through the open window. Then the girls shrieked even louder. I think Verity was *three* floors up. We laughed until our stomachs ached, but when Father came to see what was so funny, we didn't tell him. He would have had an apoplectic stroke. I think he would have had a hard time believing his Sainted Verity would pull such a lunatic stunt. I had a hard time myself. I have had to change some of my thoughts about my big sister. When I think of her edging along that ledge with no handholds, clutching a baby mouse, I get queasy. The worst part, according to her, was that if she had been seen, she would have been expelled. Imagine risking your nursing career, which really mattered to you, for the sake of a silly prank! It is the sort of thing boys are forgiven but not girls. Girls are supposed to be proper, like Florence Nightingale, who was strict about how nurses behaved. Secretly, though, I envy Verity and I am proud of her too.

Bedtime. Verity will be up to sleep with me tonight although she will have to leave very early. It is so nice to know she will be coming up any second.

Wednesday, October 10

Jack *has* been given the job of training young pilots. Well, he is being trained to teach them. Rufus is hoping to do the same thing. They flew so many missions in such a short time. Maybe the officers could tell they were growing tired. I cannot imagine Rufus being tired. But Jack says it is a terrible strain sometimes, especially on foggy nights.

School is keeping me busy. We are putting on another concert at the church to raise money to send comforts to our troops. I am going to recite "In Flanders Fields." It is a poem written by Dr. John McCrae. His family and Grandmother are friends from long ago. I saw his house when we were in Guelph. It is not a mansion, just an ordinary house.

It is such a stirring poem. But I will do it *without* Verity's hand gestures.

I still want to know about Rufus's wedding, but will be glad when I don't have so many secrets to keep. I am afraid of letting something slip out accidentally. I suppose Jack would forgive me and Rufus's commanding officers would never know.

We are so far away. If only the War would end. It has lasted over three years now. At the beginning everyone said it would be over in a few weeks. It must seem to the younger children that there never was a world without the War.

I am sure Belle cannot remember that we used to have desserts so often, before sugar was scarce — roll jelly cake, custard pie, angel food cake, apple dumplings and pound cake. How I love pound cake! And it has been months since I had a slice. I forgot to mention Devil's Food cake and English Trifle. Mmmmmm!

But whenever Moppy makes a pan of Russian toffee to send to Jack and Rufus, she gives one piece each to Charlie, Susannah and Belle. I got one too until my twelfth birthday. You never saw such interest in packages for the troops as those children show, dear Reader. I heard Belle just last night telling Moppy that poor Jack has not had a box from home for *ages!* "I'll send off some socks tomorrow, Emily Belle," Moppy said solemnly. "Just socks!" wailed Belle.

Saturday, October 13

Dear Reader, do you go to school? You must. If you do, you will understand why I keep skipping whole days. The teachers seem to pile on the work, and we have to help with the war effort too. At least we are through growing vegetables until next spring, and the War will surely be over by then.

Matthew (the boy who delivers telegrams) helped me with my Algebra today. He happened to notice I was floundering. I just do not see the sense in it. He is so nice.

I had written Jack awhile ago that I was thinking of getting my hair bobbed, even though I know Father does not like the idea. Verity's looks magnificent. Jack wrote back by return mail that he did not like the idea either. Really!

"I don't want my little sister to be all grown up when I come home," he wrote. Do they think we can keep the world exactly as they left it? Wait until he sees Aunt Martha at the wheel of her Tin Lizzie.

Yet, dear Reader, he sounded so shaken. I don't care that much about short hair. It is such a shock to find that such a detail can bother him. He must be . . . exhausted maybe, and hurt by what he faces whenever he visits the hospital.

And it can't be easy watching Rosemary with Rufus.

I'll send him a copy of Belle's poem. That will make him smile:

I would like going to church all right
If my hat elastic weren't so tight.

Grandmother is not as well as she was. Aunt M. seems worried, but she does not seem frantic.

Sunday, October 14

The newspaper reports are not so good lately. Our Canadian troops are involved in that battle at Passchendaele now. Soldiers have talked about how horses died in that mud. It was as high as the men's thighs. They were plastered with it and had nowhere they could go to get clean. It must have been nearly impossible to walk. They dared not sit down to rest in case they drowned in the muck.

Monday, October 15

I have learned "In Flanders Fields" off by heart. I am ready to recite it at the concert in support of the troops.

Wednesday, October 17

A telegram came today. Jack is wounded. A letter will follow. What does it mean, *Wounded*? It said he was in hospital. I wonder if it is the one where

Rosemary works. I hope Rufus is all right. They are always together.

I can't write any more, dear Reader. I can't. It is like Hugo all over again. A nightmare.

Only, Jack is alive!

Friday, October 19

No news.

Whoever said "No news is good news" was not waiting for word from a hospital on the other side of an ocean.

Tuesday, October 23

Dear Reader, you seem completely unreal. But you are all I have so I will write to you, unreal or not.

We are still waiting for news. All we have heard is that Jack has been burned. Father is trying to get some word from Rufus's family. Prince Rupert is so far away. Most people do not have telephones and West is a common name. There are several listed. Father also asked Dr. Webb for help in finding out more about Jack. Dr. Webb said he would do what he could, but with burn cases there might not be anything to say for a week or so until they see how he fares. Father told Mother that he had a feeling Dr. Webb was avoiding telling him something. Mother could not speak.

Same night

Dr. Webb sent several cables and now we know much more. I wish we did not know. Not knowing was hard but knowing is dreadful.

Rufus is dead.

Jack's plane crashed and he and another man were trapped inside. Rufus pulled Jack out and went back for the other man. The plane exploded before he could get him out and they were both killed. Jack was badly burned, but if it were not for Rufus he would have died.

But he is not blind and he still has his hands and feet. Mrs. Webb said we must be thankful. I suppose we must.

Dr. Webb says Rufus may be given a decoration posthumously. He said everyone agrees he deserves it.

What use is that if you are dead? Rufus's family have still not written or cabled. Father says they need time. We all need time.

Monday, November 5

Two weeks have passed with no proper letter from Jack or the hospital. Dear Reader, things keep happening and I know I ought to write them down but I feel as though I have turned to stone.

Hallowe'en came and went and the younger children hardly even noticed. You would think Jack had died. But

I just realized this is Guy Fawkes Day, but I won't remind them. Nobody cares. We don't really do anything about it anyway. It is too close to Hallowe'en.

If only Jack himself would write. He *can* write because a card came penned by him. It just said, *Dear Father and Mother, I am alive. They say I will recover. Do not worry. Save your tears for Rufus.* It did not say *Love, Jack* and it did not look like his usual writing. It was printed by a shaking hand. But someone else wrote his name and included a note to say she had guided his hand for him while he wrote, and he had been too weak to write more.

The writer added that the patient was as well as could be expected and will no doubt write himself when he has recovered his strength. He says he will not see anybody.

Maybe that was why she did not say where the hospital was. It is all so strange. I know Father and Mother are alarmed but do not know what to do.

Charlie is sure Jack will be proud of his scars. It is true that the boys have always shown off any scars they got, even when they were practically invisible. I hope Charlie is right.

I know Father longs to go to England like Dr. Webb did, but we cannot afford to pay for his passage. And nobody has asked for him, not even Jack.

We can write to Jack though. If a proper letter does not come soon I will write and tell him how badly Father needs one.

Tuesday, November 6

A nurse wrote to say Jack was unable to write himself. She said he had stopped talking to everyone but she was sure he would pull out of it soon. She said this did happen to the boys who suffered his sort of injury. But she did not describe what his sort of injury was.

It ended up: *I wish I could write more but he is grieving for his friend and has shut himself away from everyone at present, poor lad.*

That *poor lad* brought tears to all our eyes. Before this war began, I had only seen Father cry when he was laughing very hard, which he hardly ever does. Men don't cry, or they aren't supposed to. But I have seen him cry many times now, especially since Hugo was killed.

Friday, November 9

Dear Reader, I feel so old and I feel as though I am being scarred like Jack by all that is happening. Oh, I so wish you were real and I could tell you face to face what is on my mind. I got a letter from Rosemary. It is very short. I will copy it here. Then

I can throw it away. Here it is.

Dear Eliza,

Perhaps I should not write to you but I know Jack told you about me and I need to tell someone in your family what is going on here. I don't know your parents. I went over to the hospital where Jack is and tried to see him but they say he will not see anyone. His face has been badly burned and I know from experience that such injuries affect people strangely. But it sounds as though he is walling himself off from everyone. I think it is more than Rufus's death although I can't explain why I think so. But I can't get to him. Would you write, Eliza? I do need to see him. Surely he has written to you. He is so fond of his little sister. Please, ask if I can come even for five minutes.

Sincerely,

Rosemary Trent

What does it mean? What should I do?

Dear Reader, I am so worried. I wrote to Jack. I heard Mother crying and I got so mad. I am anxious about Rosemary too. So I poured out my worries about both of them in letters to them both. I told him he could not turn his back on us. I reminded him that he had promised to look after Rosemary if anything happened to Rufus. He told me so himself. Her letter sounded so lonely and worried.

I told *her* to go to wherever he was and just bash

in no matter what bosh anyone else said. I maybe should not have said any such thing.

I got an envelope and found the address for the hospital on Father's desk, and mailed Jack's letter. Was it a terrible thing to do? Oh, I am beside myself! I can't concentrate on school or the younger children.

I keep thinking about Rosemary and wondering if I should tell Father and Mother about her. But so far I have not known what to say and the right moment to speak about it all has not come.

I wrote another page to her and told her exactly what I had written to Jack and ordered her again to just bust through to him no matter what. We used to play a game where we had a secret password. I told her to send it in to him if nothing else worked. It means: Comrade, I need you. It is *Open Sesame*, spelled backwards. We had four or five secret words. I am sure he will remember. *Emases Nepo* sounds a bit silly now but it was useful when we were little.

I am afraid Mother and Father will be very angry with me for letting this secret go on for so long without saying a word. They have always said you should only keep a promise where no one would really be hurt if you broke it. It won't make them forgive me if I say I could not tell because I had promised Jack to keep his secret.

Oh, what a tangled web we weave
When first we practise to deceive.

Monday, November 26

Important goings-on in town. Prime Minister Borden spoke at the Uxbridge Music Hall today, and it seems like half the town turned out to hear him. Father went, but Mother didn't. All we can think about is Jack.

Thursday, November 29

No letters from England. I am sorry, dear Reader, not to have written. I am beside myself, as Aunt Martha says. That is a strange expression. How can a person be beside herself? But it is how I feel. Divided. Cut in two.

I am not being a faithful journal keeper, but once I start, I get into hurtful things and sometimes I start and make a muddle and tear out the page and start again.

Saturday, December 1

Still no word but my letter may have just arrived.

I suppose I should tell you of some normal happenings in our lives. Once you stop writing every day, it is hard to start up again. You, dear Reader, grow far off and faint in my mind.

But I did recite "In Flanders Fields" at the concert. It was terribly hard to do. I hated the bit, "We are the Dead. Short days ago, we lived, felt dawn, saw sunset's glow . . . " It was written up in the paper and the reporter said: *Young Eliza Bates brought tears to our eyes with her recitation.*

I don't know how I managed not to cry but I told myself it was about nobody I knew and just kept going. On the way home, nobody said a word but Mother squeezed my hand so tight it almost hurt.

We are beginning to start preparing Christmas gifts. It is not easy when you don't have much pocket money.

Tuesday, December 4

I finally heard from Rosemary again. It was mysterious, to put it mildly. I will copy it as I did with the other. She does not prattle on for pages.

Dear Eliza,

I took your advice. They were not going to let me into the ward because he had said he would not see anyone. But I sent in your password, gave him time to take it in and then just pushed the ward sister aside and made for his bed. He was holding my note, which made it easier to be sure it was him. Oh, Eliza, poor old Jack is having a rough time of it these days. He blames himself for Rufus's death. And he thinks he has turned into some sort of monster because his face is so scarred.

At first he thought he was going blind because of the bandages, but he is not. He is a brick. I think I managed to turn his mind in a new direction by telling him about my troubles and asking for his help. I knew Jack had promised Rufus to look after me if I ever needed looking after. Well, I do need help and he rose to the challenge. I can't tell you now. But you will learn soon what a honey your brother is. No wonder Rufus loved him! He said "Jack is very decent, an all around great fellow." That really means he loved him as though they were brothers.

Thanks a million for your help, Eliza. Jack and Rufus both said you were a great kid and they were surely right. I met Hugo, you know. He came to England on leave just before Vimy. He spoke of you too. He told me you were his favourite sister. That is quite a compliment from a man with four. I must go. Maybe we will have happy times together some day. They seem far off at the moment.

Write to Jack, Eliza. He needs to hear there are people out there remembering him.

Your friend,
Rosemary

I wonder why she wanted to see Jack so urgently. I mustn't be a Nosey Parker but it does make me curious. She sounded almost desperate. What help did she need?

I will write to Jack every chance I get. I will tell him about Charlie trying to make poor Isaac's ears match with flour paste he made himself. Isaac looked a sight! It is a good thing paste is not hard to wash out.

Finally Mother and Father got a proper letter from him. They look much happier, although I know they will not stop worrying over him until he is here where they can touch him and feed him and hear him speak. And hug him, of course. We'll all hug him until he begs for mercy.

Friday, December 7

There has been a terrible explosion in Halifax harbour. The newspaper headlines are full of the story. A ship called the *Imo* collided with a French one, the *Mont Blanc*, and the *Mont Blanc* was full of munitions. Many buildings are destroyed, many people killed. It will take officials weeks to sort out the number of dead and injured, the newspapers say. The only good news we can see in it at all is that 150 soldiers who had been wounded at the Front and were on their way back home to Toronto had left Halifax before the tragedy happened. But what of any other wounded soldiers who were still there, dear Reader? What if *Jack* had been coming home and got off the ship there? To think of the brave wounded men getting all the way back from the Front only to be blown up right here in Canada.

Father can only shake his head. I hope you do not live in Halifax, dear Reader.

Saturday, December 15

Dear Reader, you have to forgive my neglecting you, because today is my birthday. I am entering on my fourteenth year or, in other words, I have turned thirteen. It took a lot of explaining before I understood that. Did you know that in China you are one when you are born? If I were Chinese, I'd be fourteen today.

I got a strange present from my parents. Elocution lessons! The teacher is not the one who rolls her eyes. She has just moved to Uxbridge. Her husband is an invalid. I suppose she is a Duck but she doesn't droop or carry on about herself or act like most Ducks. She was an actress before she got married and, of course, gave up her stage career. I heard one of the regular Ducks say that about her.

Why did she say "of course"? People say such things all the time. Grandmother Bates was a Methodist before she married Grandfather and she used to say, "Of course, I became a Presbyterian." But why couldn't Grandfather have turned Methodist?

Grandmother also used to say he couldn't hold onto a tune "even if it were tied up and put in a lidded basket." She has funny ways of putting things.

As for my elocution teacher, I don't think you *must* stop acting because you marry. It would be hard, though, to take care of your house and children and be ready to play Lady Macbeth after the dishes were done. Maybe, when you marry, you need to wed a millionaire who can pay for people to clean your house and raise your children.

The others pooled their money and bought me some secondhand books. My favourite is *Jo's Boys.* I already had *Little Men*. And Grandmother gave me *Little Women* and *Good Wives* when I was ten. I got *Daddy-Long-Legs* by Jean Webster. It looks wonderful. I do so like books about orphans.

Corny gave me a present. Are you ready for a shock? She gave me a cross-stitch kit complete with a small embroidery hoop and all the thread. I said I was thrilled and I did not laugh, but Susannah almost gave me away.

"But, Eliza, you always said — " she started.

I was brilliant. I interrupted her fast and firmly and said, " . . . always said how badly I wanted a kit just like this!"

Susannah closed her lips and Corny beamed.

The Webbs are talking about making a fresh start

somewhere else, far from here. They have relatives out West and Richard might do better there. I do pray so. Corny says he'll be hunky-dory. That sounds funny applied to Richard.

Friday, December 21

This is the beginning of winter officially. It is the shortest day and the longest night. It is nice to toast our toes at the hearth fire in the evenings but I will be glad when the light begins to come back. Dark skies make gloomy thoughts harder to chase away. I try never to write to Jack when I am gloomy. I tell him the funniest and most beautiful things I can think of. I feel it is like throwing him a lifeline. Maybe I am wrong.

Sunday, December 23

Dear Reader, I am busy making some Christmas gifts. I like drawing and I decided I could make Belle a colouring book and draw some paper dolls for Susannah. It is harder than you might think. I would trace the clothes from *Vogue*, which Mrs. Webb gets, except then they do not fit the dolls. I can't seem to draw a *Vogue* doll and make her look one bit real.

Everyone says the War is nearing its end. I do not quite believe it though, because they have been saying the same thing for so long. It is strange to think that Belle cannot remember a time when there was no war. I wonder if she will forget Hugo. She was so little when he enlisted. She will know his face from photographs and lots of family stories about him. But will she really remember him the way I do? Poor Belle.

Christmas Day

Tuesday, December 25

It is Christmas morning and I do not hate my sister Verity! It is strange, when I look back, how angry I was just one year ago because they went skating without me. I wanted to strangle poor Verity. I forgave her long ago. Although I still do not relish being called an immature limpet!

So much has changed since then. Verity is so much easier to put up with now that she is a nurse. They all liked their presents, which was nice. Father and Mother gave me a big fat dictionary for my very own. Two years ago I would not have wanted such a useful present. But now I love sitting and reading it in odd moments. There are so many strange words. Dear Reader, do you know what an *ygdrasil* is? I thought I might try to learn one new word every day. Merry Christmas to you.

Later

What we hear from Jack is extremely skimpy. He has not said whether he will have to stay in hospital over Christmas. Maybe he has been with Rosemary and met her family. Neither has ever told me what happened about that secret wedding.

I wrote to him anyway and did my best not to sound reproachful.

1918

Tuesday, January 1, 1918

Happy 1918, dear Reader. I hope this one is happier than the last.

Now is the day for checking those New Year's Resolutions Verity and I wrote in our journals so long ago. I found Verity's journal in her dresser drawer after she moved out. She is too tired to have energy to keep a diary. I read over her resolutions and I think she kept hers pretty well. I kept mine, more or less, but I was careful to write resolutions I thought I might be able to keep.

Wednesday, January 2

The Webbs moved out West right after Christmas. They did not put their house on the market in case they decide life in the West does not suit them. They have rented it for a year to an older couple with middle-aged children. They come to church but they are what Moppy calls "cold fish." Not the neighbours we hoped for.

On their last Sunday, the Webbs came to church — that was a surprise — all but Richard, of course. He will be going out West with them. When we sang, Lead, Kindly Light, I saw Mrs. Webb's eyes fill up with tears during the last verse. Do you know it, dear Reader? It goes:

So long Thy power hath blest me, sure it still
Will lead me on,
O'er moor and fen, o'er crag and torrent, 'til
The night is gone.
And with the morn, those angel faces smile
Which I have loved long since, and lost awhile.

Richard is not dead, but I am sure she was thinking of him being so changed. Then I saw Dr. Webb take her hand. But they left right away after the benediction. He must have felt like the Alm Uncle in *Heidi* when he first went back to church. Some of the congregation were disappointed at not getting the chance to pat them. And make a fuss. After all, everyone knows Dr. Webb said there was no God.

Saturday, January 5

I must write back to Cornelia. She says the cows are not as great a comfort as she imagined. She's scared of them. She actually misses me. I miss her too which, once upon a time, I would not have believed. But you get fond of people when you understand them. Even the parts of them which you scorned to start with grow familiar, and even endearing.

Monday, February 4

This time my neglect of you, dear Reader, has not been my fault. We have all had whooping cough. Belle caught it first, of course, from Ellie James in her Sunday school class. But she was very generous and every one of us then caught the bug. Mother put this book away on a high shelf until I got better because she was afraid the contagion would stick to it somehow. What a scene it was! People coughing and then whooping and then bringing up their boots. The adults took turns sleeping downstairs so that somebody would get some sleep. They were all kind to us but got heartily sick of it. But today we are all recovered, at long last, and Mother gave me back my precious journal.

We got TWO letters from Jack. They were most unsatisfactory. He is not telling us things that really matter. I cannot understand it. He does say he is getting better faster than the doctors believed possible. No mention of Rosemary!

He sounds cranky and discouraged. It must be hard for him, facing the future without Rufus.

It would feel empty. And I am not the only one who misses Hugo. I must try to remember.

Thursday, March 21

It is the first day of spring. But I feel as though it is cold old November with all the winter stretching out ahead of me. Mother is keeping me home from school. She says I look peaked. I am never sure what that means but it is not good. My throat hurts and I have a headache.

Easter Sunday
March 31

On Easter Sunday morning, in our house, we greet each other with the old words, "Christ is risen." Then the person who has been greeted answers, "He is risen indeed!" I did not really learn to do it without being prompted until I was nine and I was so proud when I beat Father to it and surprised him. Yet I met him in the hall this morning and said, "Christ is risen, Father." And he didn't answer. I said it again, louder. Then he seemed to wake up and he said, “Yes, daughter. Christ is risen.” He went on down to the kitchen.

I felt tears in my eyes because he had forgotten. Oh, dear Reader, seeing him this way makes my heart ache.

Fifteen minutes later

I just heard him going to the hall mirror to check his tie and I ran out to him.

“Father, listen to me,” I said. “Christ is risen.”

And he hugged me and then held me away and said, ever so softly, “He is risen indeed, Eliza. Hallelujah!”

It was the best moment I have shared with him in a long, long time.

Tuesday, April 9

I am sorry I have written so little lately. The others got all better but I had some sort of relapse. Not contagious. But I was too weak and feeble to write. I do a bit of something and then I have to lie down. I have a fever too. It seems so much more important when you have a fever.

But I will write lots as soon as I feel up to it.

Friday, April 12

It took me so long to grow strong again and then I had all my schoolwork to catch up on. Matthew actually came over to the house to help me with Algebra and Latin. I am not fond of Latin. Matthew, in case you've forgotten, is the boy who works in the telegraph office.

As soon as I get less wobbly in the knees, I will write much more, dear Reader. Something exciting is bound to happen and inspire my faithful green pen to fountain forth.

Monday, April 15

Do you think I could possibly have the Second Sight? Something exciting has indeed happened. I think today has been the strangest and most exciting day of my life. It surely had the most exciting beginning. I will tell you every dramatic detail to make up for all the weeks I skipped.

I woke up before sunrise because I heard a burglar in the house. I told myself it was what Father calls my overactive imagination and listened hard. But the noise I had half-heard was not repeated and Isaac slept on. He has slept with me ever since I got sick.

I made myself pull the covers over my head and wait until daylight. But it was my turn to go down and put the big kettle on to boil for everybody's morning tea.

I know I am spinning this out but it is *such* a story. I went into the kitchen and saw no sign of a burglar, and I had almost forgotten about it when I had to go into the dining room for something. I took one look through the door. A man, wearing an overcoat, was asleep on the floor with his back to me.

I opened my mouth to scream and squeaked instead. Then the man raised his head and I did scream long and loud. I was looking at some sort of monster.

Father says my lungs were in fine fettle, for they brought him out of his bed in a great leap and he barked his shin on the chair. I'm glad it slowed him up a few seconds because Jack had things to tell me.

The "monster" still had on his greatcoat and he had a sofa cushion under his head. He looked dusty and unshaven in the half-light. He really did look like a tramp and I thought he must have broken into the house because Father locks the doors at night.

"Pipe down, Eliza," he said, sitting up.

It was Jack's voice. But, dear Reader, the face was not Jack's. I am so ashamed. I burst out crying and I stammered, "Jack, I'm sorry. You scared me. I thought you were a mon– tramp."

And his eyes looked into mine. He knew why I had screamed. He only looked like a tramp until he showed his poor face. Then he looked like a man in a monster mask. It was made of pink rubber and, in those first few seconds, it did not look human. An ugly scar ran from his hairline down the whole left side of his face. One corner of his mouth was twisted down and the end of one eyebrow was caught in the puckered up skin.

Yet his bright eyes were Jack's and they watched me, seeing my shock but not surprised by it. He had seen it before on other faces. He expected it, by now.

"It's all right, Eliza," he said in a tired voice. "I know what you thought. It is a frightening sight, especially when you are unprepared. I could not look in a mirror for . . . weeks."

"No," I began. "I was — "

"Hush," he broke in. "We must talk."

We both heard Mother and Father coming downstairs at a breakneck pace. My brother scrambled up and leaned toward me. He looked terrified.

"What is it?" I hissed. "What's wrong, Jack?"

"I'm married and we have a baby boy," he breathed into my ear. "Don't tell. I'll tell you later."

Father burst into the room and grabbed Jack in his arms. He crushed him in such a tight hug Jack had to gasp for breath.

"Sam, let go," Mother cried out.

But the hug had all of them in it by then and she was as bad as Father — only not as strong, of course.

I thought Father would crush him to death.

"Oh, Father," Jack got out and then everybody, Jack included, was raising such a hullabaloo that the children came on the run, not wanting to miss a second of the show.

Dear Reader, I am still feeling faint. He whispered that he would tell me everything as soon as he got a chance. But there has been no chance all this joyful day. I did manage to force the baby's name out of him while we were clearing the table after breakfast.

"Rufus Hugh," he whispered, "but we plan to call him Hugh."

Oh, what has Jack done?

After midnight

Jack is asleep. He is exhausted. I have been tossing and turning ever since he left my room. I can't sleep. I feel like a music box which has been wound too tight and will break any second. So I will write to you.

I hope you will help me make sense out of my brother's muddled story. Tomorrow I will make him tell Father and Mother and I will have to keep my wits about me or they will be completely confused. And hurt because, of course, he should have told them ages ago. They don't even know Rosemary exists.

I feel as though I'm back in Muskoka and I've just fallen off the dock into water which is over my head. I can swim, as you know, but I like to be able to touch bottom if I need to. Where Jack and Rosemary and I are, right now, is deep water.

First of all, they are married. When she got in to see him in the hospital, she needed to tell him that she was going to have Rufus's baby and she did not know what to do. She had just found out that Rufus was getting the Military Cross posthumously and she was afraid they might change their minds if they found out about his marrying her when he had been forbidden to do so.

Jack told her not to say a word. He would make it all right. After all, he had asked her to marry him before Rufus had and he still wanted to marry her.

"I told her I was stubborn as a mule's hind leg," he told me, grinning.

His scar pulled his grin crooked but it was still Jack's smile. It makes everyone smile back.

First, Jack looked for the friend who had married Rufus and Rosemary, but heard that his plane had made a crash landing and he was in hospital. Rosemary thought that meant they were jinxed but Jack would not listen to her. It took some doing but they did manage to get married. Jack was not going to be flying again. So he got permission from the very man who had refused to let Rufus do it. Jack knew he would be feeling badly for denying Rufus's request and he would give in to Jack.

This, dear Reader, is when love's young dream came a cropper, as Jack put it. Jack got out of hospital and Rosemary applied for the papers to come to Canada. And then she got cold feet. She decided taking on Rufus's wife and coming baby was too much to ask of his friend.

"Then I grew angry," Jack told me, "and said the *real* reason was that she could not stand having to see my ugly mug over the breakfast table every morning."

So they quarreled and came very close to calling off their plans.

I asked what made it come right and he laughed.

"The baby," he said. "He began to kick inside her and she got so excited that she had to let me feel how strong he was. Then . . . "

He broke off then and got this lovey-dovey look on his silly face and would not tell me any more about it.

I can't write any more now. But *something* is still wrong because Rosemary would not let him take her straight to our house. She is sure Father and Mother will not understand how it was.

I think they are crazy, dear Reader, but we will fix it all tomorrow. I must sleep.

I can hardly wait to see this baby.

Thursday, April 18

I am worn ragged and he still has not told them. He made me swear I would not burst out with the story. He will tell me when, he says.

I asked him if he was ashamed of her.

"No," he said. But Rosemary made him promise to keep it a secret.

It is all so stupid. They've been married for months and quarreling the whole time. Yet I have a funny feeling they enjoyed patching up all those spats. Do you suppose, dear Reader, this is what they mean by True Romance? I think maybe it is. If so, I am not looking forward to falling in love.

Sunday, April 21

He has not told Mother and Father, dear Reader. I cannot understand him. He is terrified that they won't love her. Why wouldn't they?

What on earth is wrong with her? She sounds jim-dandy to me.

Mother and Father are baffled, I can tell. Mother even asked Jack if he wanted to telephone Norah. She said she'd pay for the call. The light was poor where he was sitting and his scars made his face hard to read, but I saw it stiffen into a mask.

"She's not expecting to hear from me," he said. "It's all over between us. I don't want to talk about it."

Mother started to say something, but I blurted out that Aunt Martha had told me that Norah has a new beau.

"Oh, three people wrote to me to tell me how faithless my girl was," Jack said. "You'd be amazed how thoughtful people can be."

His voice was flat but not anguished so we let that subject go.

He keeps pulling Belle onto his lap and holding her as though he could not bear to let her go. I am ashamed to feel jealous of her. It is something different than jealousy. It makes me feel more alone, I think. Belle makes him laugh.

Monday, April 22

A letter came from Rosemary to Jack. "Well, well," said Father in a heavy voice. "It looked like a woman's handwriting."

"It *was*," said Mother positively. "But don't tease him, Sam. There's more here than meets the eye."

Surely he will tell them tomorrow. Father has borne enough.

Tuesday, April 23

Jack has nightmares. He woke me up last night twice. I listened to him for a bit but then, dear Reader, I went into his room. He was crying and I knew he would not want Mother or Father to know. I confess, dear Reader, I was frightened. It was nearly three in the morning. And in between the crying he kept swearing.

"Why couldn't you have kept out of it?" he said, all at once. "Why did you have to be a hero? Why did you have to shoot him?"

I think he was talking to Rufus at first, but then Rufus maybe turned into Hugo. I felt like a snoop so I pulled the light cord and went over and shook him. He sat up so fast and I think he thought I was the enemy until he realized he was in pyjamas. His eyes were huge and wild. He did not know me.

"Jack, it's me," I said. But I had to whisper because everyone was asleep. I wanted to run for Verity, but she isn't home.

Then Jack said, "Mother?"

I almost shrieked. I can't explain why that was the most frightening moment. But he was staring right at me and he did not know who I was.

"It's me. Eliza," I said. Then I started to cry. Remember about my eye going off to the side or in toward my nose? Well, it did that and his face turned into Jack's and he said, "Hello, Eliza. What's up?"

So I told him, and he told me he has bad dreams, but a lot less often than he did. Then he patted the bed just the way Mother does when we have bad dreams.

So we talked and he asked me what he had said. I told him the first part and he said he dreams he is trying to make Rufus stay back, but Rufus won't listen. He smiled then and said he was fine and I should go and get my sleep.

After I was back in bed and almost asleep, I heard him cry out again. I stayed where I was this time and waited to see what would happen. I think I was hoping Mother would go in to him. She didn't. But he woke himself up, I guess. He put a record on the gramophone and wound it up and played it softly. It was "Love's Old Sweet Song." I went back to sleep listening. When I woke up next, it was early, early morning.

I feel more sympathetic with Cornelia now. Maybe I don't quite understand her, but I see how hard it must have been having her brilliant brother come home so changed. At least Jack is still Jack, despite the scars. Maybe there are scars inside though.

It was just after five when I got up for a drink of water and heard him crying out. When I woke him, he said he was sorry to wake me again. I talked him into sneaking down to the kitchen with me and I made some cocoa.

Then he told me that Rosemary understands because she is a nurse who has seen lots of wounded soldiers. I said he should tell Mother and Father that he has a wife. He said he knows he must, but he cannot bear it if they say anything cruel about her.

"Why on earth would they? You know them better than that," I told him. Then I said if he didn't tell them, I would, promise or no promise. "How can you be afraid of facing your own parents?" I said. "I thought you were a hero."

Dear Reader, he looked at me and said, "Not me, Eliza. You have me mixed up with Rufus."

Then he cried.

You should know that Jack never cries.

I wanted to cry too and run for Mother, but stopped myself. Something told me not to baby him. I put my foot in my mouth, all the same.

"Hugo would tell them," I said.

Jack's face flushed scarlet and the tears vanished. Words spurted out of him like water out of the pump. "Oh, I know they'd forgive Hugo anything," he said in a hard tight voice. "I know as well as you that their white-haired boy could do no wrong. I'm sure they wish I'd died in his place."

Then I saw Father stopping just outside the kitchen door. He could not have chosen a worse moment. I gulped in air and plunged into speech. "Father," I said before Jack could say something disastrous. "Jack had a bad dream. If you will sit here and help him get over it, I will go and get dressed."

Then I ran up here, leaving them together.

But, oh, dear Reader, how can we help him?

Saturday, April 27

This journal is growing more and more like *Jane Eyre* and less and less like a schoolgirl's journal. Here comes another exciting bit.

I was looking out the window this afternoon and saw Matthew talking to Charlie. They looked agitated but then Charlie came running to get me because Matthew had a message he had to deliver in person. Matthew would not let Charlie hand it over. Here it is. A telegram!

ELIZA STOP LIZZIE AND I COMING TOMORROW STOP BRINGING GUESTS FROM ENGLAND STOP PREPARE ANNABELLE STOP LOVE AUNT MARTHA

Matthew's eyes bored into me. I could feel my mouth drop open. It took me only a few seconds to decode it once I knew who had sent it.

"I thought it sounded private and if one of your parents caught me, they might ask questions and you might have trouble explaining," he said, going a bit red.

I said he was absolutely right. Then he told me he had read it when it came in at the office and he was dying to know what it meant.

I am sure he is not supposed to ask questions about the telegrams he brings, but he is a really nice boy, dear Reader. I think I told you he is in my class.

If the infants had not crowded around, I would have explained the message but he grinned at me in the most understanding way.

Then I was inspired. "*Lizzie* is a friend of Mr. *Ford*," I said. "She's a fast mover."

"You mean — " he started. Then he laughed out loud.

"Like the Tin Man?" he said.

Get it? He meant Tin Lizzie? I nodded and ran in. Mother is out at a meeting so I am writing in here while I wait. I think I will have to wait even after she comes home because little pitchers have enormous ears in this house. I'll get her when they are in bed.

Fifteen minutes later

Charlie just came and said Matthew was back. He had wired Aunt Martha an answer. Here's the copy he brought me:

DEAR AUNT MARTHA STOP LOOKING
FORWARD TO SEEING YOU AND YOUR
PARTY STOP LOVE ELIZA

He is such a smart boy. I wonder how he got them to send it. He does get paid so I suppose he can afford it. Is that my first present from a boy, dear Reader? Perhaps. It is not the sort of present I thought I would get. Grandmother says you can only accept candy or flowers. I wonder what she would say about telegrams.

I never thought a telegram would make me laugh out loud.

Late, late, late

I told Mother the truth. I started in hinting and then she looked me straight in the eye and said, "Spit it out, Eliza. Is it something about Jack? I cannot bear the suspense."

"He's married," I blurted, "and he's afraid you won't like her and . . . "

"Norah?" she whispered.

"No. Her name is Rosemary. She's from England. She's coming here tomorrow."

Dear Reader, she sank down on the bed and looked very peculiar, and I meant to tell about the baby and everything but I couldn't get out the words. Then we heard Father coming up the hall.

"How is she getting here?" Mother whispered.

I told her Aunt Martha would be bringing her tomorrow.

Father came in then and stared at us as if we were conspirators — which, of course, we are. Mother just told me to run along to bed so I did. But I doubt I will sleep a wink. Jack is out late with an old friend he ran across a day or two ago. I hope he comes home and gets a good sleep. He's going to need it.

Have I betrayed him or helped him out? Well, both. But I'm not alone. Mother looked relieved when I said the girl was not Norah. I thought she liked her. I never would have guessed.

Sunday, April 28

We went to church, of course, and had Sunday dinner. But the minute I was excused from the table, I went outside to wait. Pretending to look at the birds and the budding trees while really watching for that Tin Lizzie. I knew they would not get here for hours. Jack tried to get me to go for a walk but I said we should stick around, because we might be having visitors.

He scowled. "Not a Duck, I hope. I was planning to break the news," he muttered, "but I'll take a powder if Ducks are waddling in."

Then, thank goodness, Aunt Martha pulled up in her brand new car with Rosemary beside her holding a wrapped-up bundle.

Jack almost passed out, dear Reader. So did I, even though I expected them. Then, before he could move hand or foot, Mother swept out of the house, walked straight over to the car and said, "Welcome home, Rosemary."

By the time I'd closed my mouth, Jack had sprung up, flown across the yard and had his arm around Mother's shoulders. Aunt Martha had taken the bundle. Then Rosemary climbed out.

Suddenly I heard the front door open behind me and Father stuck his head out. "Annabelle, what on earth — " he started.

I ran straight to him. I knew, in a flash, that he should not be left out, as if he were not a member of the family. I know too well how changelings feel.

"Jack's married," I said in a great rush, "and they have a baby and Aunt Martha has brought them to meet you."

Father looked at me for a long moment and told me to say that again, and say it slowly.

I did.

"Is the baby a boy?" he asked me. I wondered why that mattered, but I nodded my head.

"What's his name?" he asked.

I was taken aback but I told him. "Rufus Hugh Bates. They call him Hugh."

"Thank you, Eliza," he said. Then he turned me around so I faced the group by the car and Charlie and Susannah and Belle were there too, springing up like jack-in-the-boxes. Everyone pushed close and we walked out to join the crowd. We made quite a mob in the street.

And, dear Reader, at long last, Jack stopped looking terrified and started looking a mixture of stunned, proud and jubilant!

Oh, dear Reader, I was crazy with relief and joy and yet I was afraid too. I understood Jack's being nervous much better. What if somebody said the wrong thing?

"Come on into the house, for pity's sake," Mother said, laughing. "We're setting tongues wagging all up and down the street." The young ones all turned and waved.

By then Mother had the baby. I looked at Rosemary and I could tell she wanted to snatch him back but I knew she did not stand a chance.

"You help your wife, my boy," Father said. "Your mother and I will bring the little fellow."

He sounded too hearty, not quite like himself, but Rosemary would not notice. After that, everything was fine almost. There were a couple of strange moments. I have to think them over. But wasn't that whole scene astonishing?

I must tell you so much more, dear Reader, but I have to sleep. Also my hand is aching.

Tuesday, April 30

I don't know where Monday went. It seemed that everyone had to go back over everything and then do it again and again. But now it is done, I can finally tell you about Rosemary and her baby. She has brown hair, a bit reddish and glossy as a conker. She wears it down when she is just at home but twisted up on top of her head when she dresses up. Her nose is big but not too big. Her mouth is big too and it droops with weariness or sorrow until she looks at her baby. He almost always makes her smile. Her eyes are deep blue like the sky just when the first star comes out. She has one dimple. And she has a deep laugh that makes you want to laugh back. She is tall and strong and she has a British accent.

Well, it would be strange if she didn't. Jack teases her about it sometimes. I wish he would not. She smiles but I think it makes her feel set apart.

She has a lovely singing voice so she fits right into our singing family. I heard her singing, "Sleep, my child, and peace attend thee . . . " last night to Baby Roo.

Belle started calling him Baby Roo. He is supposed to be Hugh but I have heard Rosemary calling him Roo herself. Maybe we'll all stop when he gets bigger.

Belle hangs around Roo a lot. I wonder if she feels pushed out of her place as Family Baby. I don't think so. She doesn't get as jealous as I do.

Aunt Martha is going back to Guelph first thing in the morning. She told me it was my job to make sure Rosemary settles in happily.

"Why my job?" I asked. "Verity will be here on Friday."

"Verity is an exemplary niece," she said, "but she has not your imagination or your empathy."

I have no idea what she means but I'll be sure to look it up. I never dreamed I was better at something than Verity.

She has not met Rosemary yet, of course, or even heard of her. Knowing Jack, he is all in a dither about how they will hit it off. I personally think we dither too much. Everything seems perfect to me by now.

We *are* short of beds, but that will change as soon as Jack finds somewhere to take his family.

Friday, May 10

Dear Reader, I have been so busy with Jack and Rosemary and Roo, that I haven't written to you for ages. Verity and Rosemary did hit it off because they talked on and on about nursing. I suppose I could have felt left out, but it just gave me more time to be with Roo.

I never knew one could love a baby so much. He's not that much more than a month old. He can't walk or talk or sing or play Patty Cake. But his smile is as beautiful as a sunrise.

Our family takes up so much time, dear Reader, I

have decided I must either give you a name or stop writing to you. You seem too bloodless with no name, like one of Cornelia's paper dolls. Maybe you are Beth or Ruth. Maybe Felicity. Or Cornelia? How about Sophronsiba like Phronsie Pepper? I don't know what you look like but I know you just made a face at me.

Sunday, May 12

I am sitting with the baby. I rocked him to sleep and then put him down in his bed. I was coming along the hall when I heard Jack snap, "Oh, put him down, for pity's sake, and come for a walk. If he cries, it won't kill him."

My brother sounded fed up. He also sounded a bit frightening, as though he might blow up in a rage. He used to get that way when Hugo teased him past bearing. The next minute, they would be fighting with their fists and Father would pull them apart and send them outside. They couldn't come in again until they had made peace. I never thought Jack would speak to Rosemary like that.

When she answered him, she sounded miserable.

"I don't want to leave him," she started.

I could hear the tears in her voice. Then I heard myself saying I would rock him until he dropped off, if she liked.

"Oh, Eliza, would you?" she said, as if she were on a desert island and I were a ship coming to rescue her.

Jack scooped the baby out of her arms and handed him over and next thing I knew, they were on their way down the stairs.

Mother came to the door and asked if I needed help. I could tell she wanted to take over but I was having a lovely time. "I'm fine and so is Roo," I said.

He settled down and then he stretched out stiff and his face got red and the smell was awful! Oh, dear Reader, how I wished I had given him to Mother. But I managed to clean him up. How extremely disgusting babies can be! He went to sleep after I made him sweet and clean again. Then I actually rinsed out the mess.

Am I not a superlative aunt? That's one of those new words I vowed to learn. I've only learned about seven, but never mind. How do you like *bamboozle* or *pulchritude*? It isn't always easy working them into a sentence. Did you know that *sinister* really means left-handed?

Monday, May 13

Tonight Rufus's parents came for a visit. His father was attending a conference in Toronto and visiting some relatives, so his mother came along too. They decided they would make the trip here to see Rufus's friend. It was hard to meet them, but we all tried to be comforting and show how we had loved Rufus. Then Rosemary came in with the baby and Mrs. West said, "Oh, my, what a darling little fellow."

Rosemary smiled but she had tears in her eyes.

Jack reached out for little Rufus Hugh and snuggled him close. "Well, we can be thankful he doesn't look like me," he said, grinning his crooked grin.

He actually made a joke out of the way he looks, which brought a big lump into my throat.

Then the baby gave a gurgle of laughter, because we did, and put his hand up and batted Jack's cheek and Jack kissed his tiny fingers.

Dear Reader, Roo does not even see the scars. He just sees his daddy. And he loves him so. I felt happier at that moment than I have in weeks.

They have only told me and Mother and Father about Rosemary being married to Rufus for those few days. I am not sure how they decided it but I think it was for Rufus Hugh's sake. I heard Rosemary telling Mother once that he will have enough to contend with, with his family being on two sides of an ocean. She did not mention Jack's scars but she did not need to. I asked Mother if they weren't going to tell Rufus's parents and she said, "It is not up to you and me, Eliza. Our job is to support them no matter what they decide. I would guess that they will tell them some time, but remember that they are complete strangers to Rosemary. Maybe our family is more than enough to adopt at the moment. We are quite a mob."

"Not so many compared to the Wesleys," I said.

Tuesday, May 14

This morning Rosemary looked out the dining room window and said that the daffodils are finished blooming in her parents' garden in Sussex, but we still have snowdrifts in the corners.

"But here you still have the last of the daffodils to look forward to," I told her.

She laughed that lovely laugh of hers. "You are a grand little sister, Madam Eliza," she said.

I could feel myself blushing. She has a sister, Winifred, who is my age, and she says she misses her, so I suppose I am a comfort to her.

But we surely are crowded. There just is no room for a new family, especially one so young.

I used to think Hugo was the brother who understood me best, the one I loved most — and that was true. But I know now that Jack mattered more to me than I ever guessed. Maybe I shut him out back then, always looking to Hugo. When I saw Rosemary gazing at him lovingly, I knew how much he mattered to me too.

But I have suddenly realized that I do have another brother. Charlie. Maybe he needs special loving with Roo stealing Jack's attention the way he does. I'll have to try to help. Susannah is his great comfort though.

When Verity was here I heard her ask Mother what she thought of Jack's having married Rosemary without a word to anyone.

"I think it was sneaky," she mumbled, not looking at Mother.

Mother gave her one of those looks of hers, seeing straight through to her heart. "I am so proud of Jack," she said quietly. "Rosemary is a dear girl. Now how about helping me fold the sheets, daughter."

Verity looked confused. But she got to work like a good nurse should when the matron speaks.

Friday, May 24

A baby fills up moments which should go to my dear Reader — that is why I have not written much lately. Also more schoolwork. High school is harder, that is certain. But my marks in English Composition are much higher. I have Grandmother and you to thank for that.

We are studying Shakespeare too. My vocabulary is increasing by leaps and bounds.

There is not an enormous amount of room left in this book and I would like to end when the War ends, or on Christmas Day. I also am going to a C.G.I.T. camp this summer. It stands for Canadian Girls in Training and we just started a group here. We have a uniform. We wear middy blouses and dark skirts. You know I like wearing middies. It will be fun meeting new girls who have not known Cornelia and Richard and my brothers. I won't have to keep explaining to them.

Wednesday, May 29

It has been a difficult day for Uxbridge, Dear Reader. In April we heard that Colonel Sam Sharpe from the 116th was going to be coming back home on leave, but he didn't even make it here. He got as far as Montreal, and had to go into hospital, and a few days later he was dead. I don't know all the details, but there has been a lot of whispering about it. So many of the men from the 116th have been wounded or killed in the last while, it must have been very hard on Colonel Sharpe, maybe more than he could bear. It has been terrible for the people here in town. There are black armbands everywhere.

Today was Colonel Sharpe's funeral and just about the whole town turned out to watch the procession pass.

It is so sad that he almost but didn't quite make it home. What a tragedy.

Saturday, September 21

Poor, neglected dear Reader, I let months pass without a word. The Spanish Influenza has struck at even the people in Uxbridge. It seems so hard after all we have been through with the War.

The schools in Toronto are closed, though ours here in town are still open. They say people are dying as if this were another war and disease were the enemy instead of the Kaiser. Verity is not training now but nursing flu victims full-time. Mother worries about her coming down with it, but Verity herself says she's strong as an ox and don't fuss. Aunt Agnes and her husband both contracted it and nearly died but pulled through. A niece of his did die. I barely knew her. She was twenty-two.

This time I have a good reason for leaving such a long gap. All summer long, my journal was lost. I put it away before I went to C.G.I.T. camp and it vanished. I could not find it when I came home. It had fallen down behind a shelf in the wardrobe and was standing on its edge up against the wall, and did not show up until Moppy did a gigantic turning out of all the cupboards. Now it will have enough pages left, I am sure, so that I can make it to Christmas.

I enjoyed that camp, by the way, and I made a couple of friends, but they don't live here and I have not seen them since. I have written to them but neither of them likes writing.

A great change came about in the family a month ago. Aunt Martha asked Jack and Rosemary if they would like to come and take care of Grandmother while she, Aunt M., goes to Business College. We were all flabbergasted. But it has solved so many problems. Jack is getting well again there and becoming a great father.

Aunt Martha can now type one hundred words a minute. She even looks different, but I don't know how to explain this change.

Monday, October7

The War is not yet over but Jack says the victory is sure now, and it is only a matter of time. The Canadian soldiers made that big push at Amiens in the summer and that seems to have turned the tide. Father has put a big pin in his map at Amiens, and at Bourlon Wood and Cambrai. Jack says we really have the Germans on the run now, but he is saddened that the casualties are so high. I think of other families losing sons and brothers, feeling as we did after Vimy. It is so cruel for death to come just as you thought it was over.

ARMISTICE DAY

Monday, November 11, 1918

I saved a few pages of my journal for this event.

Hugo promised me it would end and we would win and he was right. He also said he would come home safe and sound and he didn't. I am sure he tried his best.

Now for the grand announcement . . . Listen to the fanfare of trumpets!

THE GREAT WAR IS OVER!

It is so wonderful, and yet so sad that Hugo is not here to celebrate. They signed the Armistice at eleven o'clock on the eleventh day of the eleventh month. We knew it was coming, but we did not get the actual news until late in the day. Oh, dear Reader, it is over at last.

People in town just poured into the streets when the Armistice was finally announced. All that anticipation people had been feeling just spilled right out of the houses. The streets were so crowded you could barely walk along them. Bells were ringing. Somebody started a little victory parade and others joined in. Cars were going along the street with people hanging off the sides. People lit a big bonfire right in the middle of town. There has been much sadness to bear, and the revelry was just what people needed.

Moppy said, "There'll be sugar aplenty before we know it! You can have pound cake for your birthday, Eliza."

I love pound cake, but I was surprised that it was the first thing she thought of.

Charlie said, "Does it mean no more weeding the garden?" How funny of him when it is November to think of next summer.

Moppy was still going on about making my pound cake.

"There won't be much sugar in the store yet," Father said, laughing at her. "At least, not at a decent price."

"I know, I know," Moppy said, "but imagine it."

Another friend of Jack's was injured a month ago. It seems more tragic because it was so close to the Armistice. Father says people will be killed even after the War officially ends.

One of the Ducks from church came over after supper and said, "It is such a joy that the fighting is done at last and we can put it behind us and forget."

She beamed around at us, but none of us said a word. For us, it will never be all over. Hugo died. Jack was changed into somebody else. Rosemary lost Rufus. None of it can be put right.

But there will come a day when no more will die. That is a good reason to celebrate even while we remember.

And it has not been all tears. Verity has become a nurse. I am an aunt. Most of us escaped Spanish Influenza. Belle learned to read. She read *The Little Red Hen* to me last night without a single mistake. And Christmas is only a little over a month away. Maybe a family with children will buy the Webbs' house, now that they have decided to settle out West and put it up for sale. Several people have been to look at it. Charlie says they think it is haunted, but Richard did not die. He is supposed to be doing better now they are out West. I wonder if Cornelia did end up with a calf to cosset.

Wednesday, December 4

A family is coming to live next door. The father is taking over Dr. Webb's practice. He came yesterday. The family is moving in when school closes for the Christmas holidays. Nobody seems to know how many children or how old they are. Father has met the father and says he seems a fine fellow, but Father never asks the right questions. He is as irritating as Mr. Bennet in *Pride and Prejudice.*

There is a lot of painting and papering going on. It is exciting. The children keep spying out the windows and reporting every new development.

Friday, December 6

Susannah and Isaac saw a cat looking out the bay window next door. A big marmalade one. I don't know which of them was more excited. The cat was calm. Susannah says it has golden eyes, but how she could see that from our house, I cannot fathom. Mother must have wondered too.

"Susannah, no spying on the neighbours," she said.

It is a little late to be giving that order.

Tuesday, December 17

We are so busy getting ready for Christmas that I hardly have time to write a word. Such cooking as you cannot imagine! And a concert at Sunday school, a choir one and a school one. Oh, dear Reader, I have only a few pages left to fill. I think I will save the last bit until Christmas Day so I can end where I began.

Christmas Day

Something strange and wonderful has happened and I still cannot believe it. I think I have found you, dear Reader. I was letting Isaac out this morning when, all at once, I heard something which froze me where I stood. It was a tune played on a penny whistle. The next instant I was running down the steps into the garden and staring over the hedge. There under the big oak tree in the Webbs' front lawn stood a girl.

It was you, Tamsyn. I thought of so many names for my dear Reader, but I never once thought of Tamsyn.

You had found my whistle caught deep in the hedge. It was not on the ground or near the top, as I thought it must be, but wedged in among some dead branches which were tangled up in a tight knot in the middle, so no wonder I missed it.

"Hello," you said, holding it out. "I'm Tamsyn Taylor. We moved in last night and I just found this. It was dusty but I've wiped it with my hanky and it still plays. Is it yours?"

I walked over to you and took it and I said, "It's a whistle to banish the dark. My brother Hugo gave it to me when I was five. It doesn't *really* banish the dark, but it helped me not to be afraid. I threw it away when he was killed at Vimy and then, when I tried to find it, I couldn't."

When I finished, your eyes had tears in them. You told me about your cousin Edward who died of his wounds at Ypres away back at the beginning, when we were little girls who still thought war was gloriously exciting. I didn't cry, but I felt as though we had been friends for years instead of just minutes. I was shivering but I could not bear to go back inside.

You and I are almost exactly the same age. And you have a big family too.

"They call me Monkey, short for Monkey in the Middle," you said, laughing.

I did not tell you Hugo's nickname for me, not yet. But I must have gasped. There are not seven of you, just five, two older and two tiny.

I have finished this journal, but I will keep it forever. You can read it if you want to. After all, dear Reader, I wrote it for you. I already know you like to read. I felt a jump of joy when you told me about reading *Nobody's Girl* and crying. I felt a pang, too, remembering poor Cornelia who would not understand crying over a story.

The notes of the penny whistle sounding in the garden eased the emptiness inside me. Did you know you were playing "Taps"? Maybe it is a message from Hugo.

All is well.
Safely rest.
God is nigh.

What Became of Them All

After the Great War, life gradually improved for the Bates family. Eliza stuck to her resolve to train as a teacher. She taught fifth grade and loved it. When she was twenty-four she was asked to tutor a handicapped boy who was the son of a minister. He was a widower whose wife had died of tuberculosis. Eliza fell in love with the boy's father and eventually married him — becoming, to her horror, a minister's wife. Although she never had children of her own, she and her stepson loved each other dearly. Her husband's congregation grew fond of her even though she seldom invited "Ducks" to supper. (She did rescue stray animals, and anyone visiting the manse would come away covered with dog hair.) Eliza's laughter and unfailing kindness made her popular anyway, especially with the young people in the church.

Although Eliza lost touch with Cornelia Webb before she finished high school, she and her "dear Reader," Tamsyn, became close friends. Even after they moved away from each other they wrote letters back and forth all their lives.

After the War, Verity went overseas to work with war orphans. She did not marry until she was middle-aged, and then she astonished everyone by wedding a Belgian doctor with whom she had worked. They settled in Europe but managed to visit Canada whenever they could afford the passage.

In 1929 Charlie emigrated to New Zealand and Susannah went along to keep house for him. She married a sheep rancher there and had twin girls. Her husband was killed in a flash flood seven years after they were married, but she and Charlie lived together happily. At the outbreak of World War II he went overseas with a New Zealand regiment. Susannah looked after the twins and the sheep until Charlie returned to her in 1946 without a scratch and with a decoration for bravery.

Belle grew passionately fond of music and determined to become a concert pianist. She lacked the stamina to make her dream come true, however, and she ended up giving piano lessons to children. They adored her. She never married, but stayed home and, after her mother's death, she and Moppy kept house for her father.

The baby, Rufus Hugh, was always a great favourite with his grandfather. He surprised everyone by turning into a brilliant scholar and eventually entering the ministry. He became a famous preacher and a grand storyteller.

Jack and Rosemary's younger son, John, loved the land and grew up to take over the family farm. Rosemary also had a little girl whom she named Eliza Winifred, after her two sisters.

After the war ended, Rev. Sam Bates was a favourite with men who had returned from the Front, especially those who had suffered injury or those so haunted by their memories that they had trouble returning to peacetime life. He did not glorify their experiences, but listened with patience and sympathy to their stories of suffering and fear, comradeship and loss, love of home and love of vanished friends. Families whose sons were comforted by him became staunch supporters of the minister.

When the Presbyterian church of Canada officially joined the United Church in 1925, Rev. Bates supported the new church. His congregation voted to stay out of Church Union, however, and joined those Presbyterians who elected to break away from the main church and form themselves into the Continuing Presbyterian Church.

After the long war years, Sam Bates was weary. He retired and he and his family left Uxbridge to move back to Guelph. They had many old friends there and they could be close to Jack and Rosemary and their growing family.

Annabelle Bates died of a ruptured appendix in 1938, eight years after Eliza's marriage. By the time she would admit that something serious was wrong and would go to the hospital, it was too late to save her. Her children and grandchildren missed her sorely. Eliza chose for her epitaph "Her light still shines."

Aunt Martha became a bookkeeper in an insurance company. She was finally persuaded to give up driving her latest car when she was eighty-two.

Historical Note

When I was a child, dear Readers, my history book told me that World War I began one summer afternoon in Sarajevo when the Archduke Franz Ferdinand was shot. I did not question this startling fact. I even believed it. But it needs to be seen in context, since many factors led up to that flashpoint. Throughout history, nations have schemed to get more land or more oil or a route to the sea or more wealth or power. Wars are also ignited by the breaking and making of alliances, and prior to World War I there was a web of these between various European nations.

England and France had been enemies in the past, but England had pledged support to France in the event of a war with Germany. When Franz Ferdinand, the Austro-Hungarian archduke, was killed by a Serb, Austria-Hungary declared war on Serbia, even though the Serbs had tried to make amends following the assassination. Russia then declared war on Austria. This dragged in Austria's ally, Kaiser Wilhelm of Germany, who then declared war on Russia. So while the assassination of the archduke was not the beginning of the trouble, it was the signal for the troubles to erupt into violence.

Kaiser Wilhelm of Germany sent his troops into Belgium, a country he had promised not to invade, and which was officially neutral. Britain gave him three days to back out. He did not, and Britain declared war. Suddenly Austria-Hungary, Germany and the Ottoman Empire (Turkey) — the Central powers — were squared off against the Allies: Great Britain, France and Russia. In no time flat other countries were drawn in and war was declared. They all believed the fighting would be over in a matter of months.

In Canada, young men poured into recruitment offices. A high percentage of Canadian families, at that time, had emigrated from the British Isles. Young men looking for a new land filled with adventure and offering a fresh start had been turning to Canada since the end of the nineteenth century. These young people were enormously loyal to Britain and felt compelled to defend their motherland. They rushed to enlist. Prime Minister Robert Borden said that Canada must stand with Great Britain, and Opposition leader Wilfred Laurier, ever the orator, echoed Borden's sentiments. "When the call comes," he said, "our answer goes at once, and it goes in the classical language of the British answer to the call of duty: 'Ready, aye. Ready!'"

Many young men saw the war as a chance for a big adventure. Nobody dreamed it would be over four years before peace would return. Nobody guessed how many hundreds of thousands of young people would die or suffer mutilation before that peace would be won. "The War to end all wars" they called it, and "the Great War." They would have been profoundly shocked to learn that just over twenty-one years after the Armistice was signed, Canada would be engaged in World War II. If they had been able to see into the future, would they have thought things over and negotiated a more lasting peace? We cannot know, but it is worth pondering.

Men who did not enlist came under great pressure. Those of you who have read L.M. Montgomery's books will remember the scene in *Rilla of Ingleside* where Walter Blythe is sent a white feather, branding him as a coward and "a slacker." The Uxbridge newspaper ran an ad urging people to report any young man who was not doing his duty. Those who wrote in, telling of such a man, did not even need to give their names. The newspaper promised to see to it that all would be sought out.

One of the first county battalions to form, the 116th from the Uxbridge area, was recruited by Colonel Sam Sharpe, the local member of parliament. The 116th had deployed to England in July of 1916, before Eliza's family moved to Uxbridge. The town was immensely proud of them and followed their exploits closely throughout the war years. Many such battalions were disbanded upon reaching England and the men reassigned to other units of the Canadian Expeditionary Force (CEF), but the 116th stayed together throughout the bitter years to come. The list of names on the wall of the St. Andrew's-

Chalmers Presbyterian Church includes those of men who died in the war, names like George Clark, Russel Gould, Norman Mair, Archie Page. Newspapers reported that Colonel Sharpe's sudden death in Montreal in 1918 was a suicide — he was very close to the men he had led overseas, and perhaps could not face coming back to Uxbridge.

Any minister with pacifist leanings, like my character Sam Bates, would have had a hard time serving there at that time. Most people had no doubt that God was on the Allies' side and prayed He would punish the Germans for their atrocities and give us the victory.

Many men who had already enlisted, and some who planned to enlist, travelled to a huge military camp in Valcartier, Quebec, where they prepared to deploy overseas. The first contingent of Canadian soldiers sailed from Quebec City for England in October, 1914. The men were eager to go, fearing that if they were delayed, the war might be over before they got there. Many of the troops spent an extremely wet winter on Salisbury Plain, quartered only in tents. There they drilled and waited to be sent over the Channel into France and Belgium to face "the Hun" — a catch-all term for the enemy. Soldiers were outfitted with the Ross rifle, a Canadian-made weapon which jammed so often after repeated firing that eventually it was replaced with the British Lee-Enfield — much to the dismay of Canada's Minister of Militia and Defence, Sam Hughes, who had recommended the Ross rifle.

The first major battle in which Canadian troops played a decisive part was the Second Battle of Ypres, which began in April of 1915 and continued throughout May. French troops were facing the Germans on April 22 when the Germans fired off cylinders filled with chlorine gas. A great yellow cloud went up, choking the unsuspecting French troops. The men fell back, gasping for breath; British reserve divisions filled the gap.

On April 24 the Germans again used gas, this time against the Canadians — Winnipeg's 8th Battalion, Royal Highlanders of the 13th Battalion from Montreal and Toronto's 15th Battalion. Dr. Naismith, a chemist, advised soldiers to "Piss on your hankies, boys," and cover their noses and mouths — urine would help weaken the gas. Worse than the gas was German shelling, which devastated the shallow, muddy trenches. The 15th was hardest hit but the Canadians retreated slowly, fighting their way back to the reserve line. The cost was tremendous — 6000 dead and wounded of the 12,000 Canadian troops actually engaged — but the British commander-in-chief gratefully reported that "the Canadians had saved the situation."

On May 2, 1915, a surgeon from Guelph named John McCrae lost his closest friend in a battle in Belgium's Flanders region. In the days that followed he wrote "In Flanders Fields." This moving poem, another Canadian legacy from Ypres, is the reason we buy poppies every November to pin on our coats. In the battlefields of Flanders, once known for its wild poppies, there was really more mud than flowers.

The Battle of the Somme was a massacre that will never be forgotten in Canadian history, especially by the people of Newfoundland. On July 1, 1916, nearly 800 men of the 1st Newfoundland regiment answered roll call. That day they were ordered to charge across a stretch of ground at Beaumont-Hamel. German wire, uncut, channeled the troops into a killing ground where German machine-gunners lay waiting. They shot the Newfoundlanders down as they advanced. When the terrible smoke of gunfire cleared, the field was strewn with the dead and dying. The following morning, only 68 men were able to show up for roll call. All the rest were dead or wounded.

In Newfoundland, that day is regarded as the darkest in the island's history. The most sickening part of it was that the men died for no glorious victory, though they fought so gallantly. Their actions gave them a reputation for showing stubborn and staunch courage under attack. When I read about this battle, it reminded me of boys playing tug-of-war — pulling back, straining forward. But these "boys" were not playing a game and their war was lethal.

I have chosen this moment to insert a reminder to you, dear Readers. There are so many thousands of casualties in these accounts of famous battles. It is almost impossible to remember that each thousand was made up of hundreds of individual men like Hugo and Jack and Rufus. But stop and consider those boys from Newfoundland killed in one day in July, 1916. How many people go to your school? Probably a few hundred. Imagine all of them plus yourself lined up for assembly. Now, imagine lining up the next morning and finding that, out of every row of ten, eight or nine are missing. The others are either dead or terribly wounded. Some have been blinded, others have lost limbs. If your school had been fighting in the Battle of the Somme that day, you would have lost almost all your friends. It is no wonder that, in Newfoundland, the date on which the rest of Canada celebrates Canada Day is not a day of celebration, but one of remembrance — Memorial Day, in honour of those Newfoundland soldiers.

In early April of 1917 the Americans joined the Allies and gave their support to the cause, though it would still be many months before American troops actually landed on Europe's soil. But their involvement was needed, since the Germans were making ever more headway, and the Allied troops had suffered huge losses.

The next, and probably most famous, battle in which the Canadian forces engaged was the Battle of Vimy Ridge. One veteran said of this bitter fight, "we went up the Ridge as Albertans and Nova Scotians. We came down Canadians." Vimy was a long, low ridge of land controlled by the Germans. The British had tried to capture it, and failed. So had the French. It had defeated every Allied attempt to capture it until the Canadians arrived.

The officers planned their assault for weeks. They made a large model of the ridge and made sure everyone who was taking part in the attack knew the terrain better than he knew the back of his hand. They tunneled underground and had miles of secret pathways lit by strings of electric lights. Under the command of Sir Julian Byng, the troops drilled and drilled until they all knew exactly how the assault would go.

For months, too, Canadians "spotted" each German gun emplacement. Colonel Andy McNaughton, a McGill professor in peacetime, used microphones to locate them when they fired. For a week before the attack, Allied artillery pounded the Germans, destroying their guns and trenches, leaving the defenders hungry, thirsty and exhausted. Then the guns fell silent. Suddenly, before dawn on Easter Monday, April 9, 1917, a huge barrage fell on Vimy Ridge. Canadian soldiers hurried through tunnels, and into lightly falling snow. All four Canadian divisions advanced to take the ridge, but even the preparations could not prevent terrible losses — 10,000 Canadian casualties, 3600 of them dead.

Despite the many casualties and deaths, Vimy remains a battle that gave the Canadian army a great sense of oneness and pride. Even today, as this book is written, a few veterans are still alive to hold their heads high when they say they took part in the capture of Vimy Ridge. Many hoped this victory would turn the tide and signal the end of the war to end all wars, but such was not the case. As I have Eliza's father say, "It is easy to start a war; finishing one is another matter."

By August, 1917, a Canadian officer, Arthur Currie, commanded the Canadian Corps. Asked by his British commander to capture the mining town of Lens, Currie went to assess the situation. If he took Lens, the Germans could rain fire down from the surrounding hills. If he took Hill 70, the high ground on the approach to Lens, he could harry the Germans holding the city. They would have to capture it back, whatever the cost. So Currie took the hill. As the Germans counter-attacked, thousands fell to Canadian shells and machine guns. Stripped to the waist in the hot sun, Canadian gunners kept firing, even when German mustard gas burned their skin and lungs. Finally, the Germans had suffered enough; the Canadians held their strategic position.

The next battle the Canadians helped to turn from a defeat into a victory was Passchendaele. It was fought over a stretch of low-lying land which heavy rains had turned into a mud soup. Some men waded through black muck up to their waists. Many drowned in the mud before anyone could go to their aid. Horses fell in the mire, sank and were lost without a trace. Gun emplacements vanished into the ooze and the men nearby were helpless. When General Currie was called upon to save the situation he argued long and hard, claiming that a victory was near impossible. The British High Command could not be moved to abandon their plans, partly because the Allies were desperate for a victory. Some French and Russian troops had even mutinied, and the Germans had to be kept engaged. Currie called for wooden platforms and lightweight railway tracks to carry people across the morass.

In the end the Canadians won the ground, but bore over 15,000 casualties, a terrible price to pay. Prime Minister Borden told the British prime minister that if he was asked to send Canadian troops into another Passchendaele, he would refuse, and not another Canadian would leave our shores to come to the aid of the Allies.

Following the Russian Revolution in the fall of 1917, the new Communist government under Vladimir Ilyich Lenin chose to make peace with Germany and pull out of the conflict, deserting the Allied cause. This was a grave concern for the Allies, since now the Germans could pull back their troops from the eastern front and move all their forces to the western front. The Americans had entered the war on the Allied side none too soon.

The armies fought on throughout the spring of

1918, with the Germans penetrating deep into Allied positions. The British, the Portugese, the French — all lost ground. Posted in front of Vimy Ridge, the Canadian Corps was not attacked. In August they joined the Australians in front of Amiens. Aircraft flew overhead to drown the noise of tanks and guns moving into position. Without warning, on August 8, the Allied soldiers attacked. Together, the Canadians and Australians rolled forward thirteen kilometres, and kept going. German General von Ludendorf called it "Die Katastrophe," the "black day of the German army." General Currie then insisted on switching fronts before the Canadian advance got bogged down. On more familiar ground, Canadians shattered the Hindenberg Line, battled across the Canal du Nord and captured Cambrai. The "Last Hundred Days" cost Canada 40,000 dead and wounded but it helped end the horror. At the Armistice on November 11th, the Canadians re-took the Belgian town of Mons, where the British had begun to fight in August, 1914. A plaque there reads: *Here was fired the last shot of the Great War.*

Europe was not the only theatre of war, of course, although it was the place where most Canadian troops saw action. Allied armies clashed with Central armies in both Africa and Mesopotamia. Over 40,000 Allied soldiers were killed on the shores of Turkey in 1915, trying to take Turkish forts at the Dardanelles, with Australian and New Zealand troops bearing losses of over 10,000 men. British liason officer T.E. Lawrence became known as the legendary Lawrence of Arabia, as he and his Arab partners used what we might now call guerrilla tactics to harry Turkish troops in the desert through 1916–1918. British General Edmund Allenby led troops in Palestine and succeeded brilliantly in driving the Germans out of their desert strongholds. In December of 1917 his forces drove the Turks from the Holy Land and freed Jerusalem from Turkish control.

Battles were fought at sea as well as on land. German U-boats were able to blockade Britain, making imported goods scarce, and threatening merchant shipping as well as military vessels. In June of 1918 a U-boat sank a Canadian hospital ship, the *Llandovery Castle*, machine-gunned the lifeboats and killed most of the fourteen nursing sisters aboard.

The battle of Jutland off the coast of Denmark in 1916 had pitted the British and German fleets in a massive confrontation. Though the British fleet sustained greater losses — over 6000 casualties, plus battleships, cruisers and destroyers — the German fleet suffered enough damage to stop the Germans from risking another major confrontation at sea.

The war in the air was also gallant and filled with terror and moments of glory. The British public was terrified of the night-flying German Zeppelins. The Royal Naval Air Service was charged with intercepting them, along with German planes that crossed the English Channel to inflict damage on British shores. The Royal Flying Corps defended England as well, and its pilots in Europe flew reconnaissance to advise Allied gunners where to fire to take out German weapons or troops. The two services were combined in 1918.

Up to a quarter of Royal Flying Corps pilots were Canadian. Most famous of these was Billy Bishop. Bishop was not a great pilot but he was a great marksman, and is credited with shooting down 72 enemy planes. He was not the pilot who ended the life of Germany's famous Red Baron, Manfred von Richthofen, however. Another Canadian, Roy Brown, was given credit for that, although other research leans towards the theory that Richthofen's plane was hit by Australian ground fire instead of being shot down by Brown.

These pilots were the daredevils, the war's romantic heroes and, because so many were shot down, were looked upon like the knights of old riding forth to die. Their reputation for incredible courage lured other young men into becoming pilots. Flying was still very new then — except for the war, people at that time could go months, even years, without seeing a plane in the sky. As late as 1937, I remember running out of the house because a plane was flying over our house in Taiwan. It was still a wonder. In the early days of flying, pilots were more at risk from their own aircraft crashing, or from bad weather, than they actually were from being shot down.

The war took its toll at home too. Imported foods such as sugar were scarce, prices rose steeply, and the government urged people to cut back on using meat. You can witness most of this struggle through Eliza's eyes as she recorded it in her journal.

What changed was the feeling that war was a high adventure. What also altered, for all time, was the picture of women, secure and protected in their homes, untouched by the cruelty of far-off battles. During the war the struggle for women's suffrage, which had gone on for years, moved forward rapidly when women were needed to take the place of the men away at the Front. Women had been told they belonged in the home, rocking the cradle and getting the meals ready. Now they were running the family business, working in the fields, taking over the switchboards, running the office and so on. When the men returned, it was too late to order their wives back to their previous lives. Women knew how the world worked and they were ready to make decisions and mark their ballots. Women like Aunt Martha also started to drive cars — even to fly planes. The exploits of flyers like Amelia Earhart and Anne Morrow Lindbergh fascinated the public.

In 1918 my mother was sixteen when she applied to medical school at the University of Toronto. Men who would earlier have mocked women seeking to qualify as doctors now had a different point of view. These men had left home, served in the trenches and watched nurses working to save soldiers' lives. They had learned that their former ideas were no longer suitable, and many treated women with new respect. Male medical students gave up chanting "She doesn't know that her degree should be M.R.S. and not M.D." Men began to treat the young women more as equals. The changes for women rippled through all levels of society. Servant girls could now make better choices for themselves. The ongoing lack of a sufficient pool of servants ultimately led to the development of labour-saving household equipment.

L.M. Montgomery was a young woman during World War I. Later, using her own diaries for background, she wrote *Rilla of Ingleside.* If you want to know more about how it felt to be young and living in Canada during that agonizing war, read her novel. Maud Montgomery was a Presbyterian minister's wife and she lived, at that time, just a few miles from Uxbridge. Her diaries were an enormous help in my research for Eliza's journal.

All wars are brutal and filled with anguish. Eliza's war is still remembered as one of the worst. And summaries of war, such as this one, can be haunting. We are almost numbed as we read of battles won, lives lost. Let us also remember the valour as well as the squalor of the first world conflict, and never forget all those young people lost to our country.

The character of Hugo was inspired by the author's uncle, Lieutenant Gordon Smith Mellis Gauld. Gordon was a university student who enlisted in the Canadian Expeditionary Force. He was killed when his plane went down in March of 1918, just eight months before the War ended.

The 116th Battalion from Uxbridge marches through town before embarking for England. Those in the foreground are the signal section, bearing their semaphore flags rolled.

A battalion leaving for overseas service, 1915. Railroad platforms would be filled with loved ones saying goodbye.

The First Canadian Army at Quebec's Valcartier camp, returning from drill. Though this scene looks very orderly, the camp was formed so rapidly that the arrival of new recruits often caused massive confusion.

Canadian troops on England's Salisbury Plain parade before King George V.

A Canadian soldier peers over the top of a front-line trench in France, 1916.

Exhausted-looking Canadian soldiers returning from the trenches during the Battle of the Somme, 1916.

Canada Food Board posters such as this one urged people at home to grow their own food, to eat less meat, and to refrain from hoarding foods such as wheat and sugar.

Rain-soaked fields, such as this one near Passchendaele, left men, horses, weapons and machinery stuck in the mud.

Billy Bishop, seated here in a Nieuport, was Canada's top ace, with a total of 72 enemy planes downed.

Nurses outside Toronto's Hospital for Sick Children, 1916.

Canadian troops returning from Europe to Halifax aboard H.M.T. Olympic, *1919.*

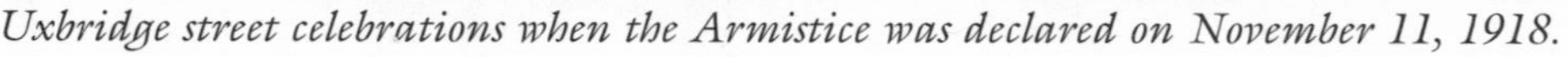
Uxbridge street celebrations when the Armistice was declared on November 11, 1918.

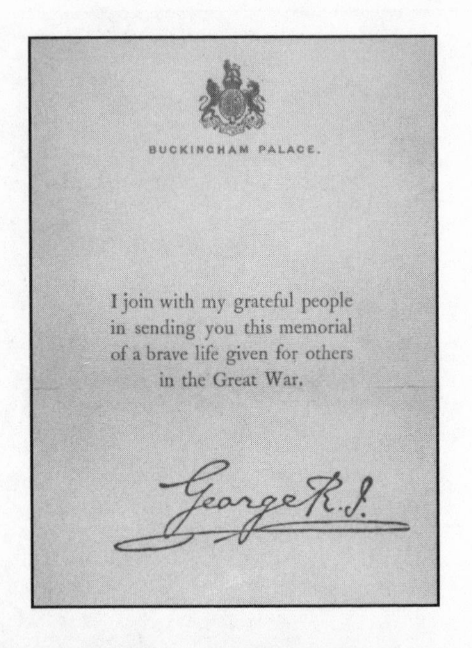

BUCKINGHAM PALACE.

I join with my grateful people
in sending you this memorial
of a brave life given for others
in the Great War.

George R.I.

THE PRESIDENT'S OFFICE
UNIVERSITY OF TORONTO
April 17, 1918.

Dear Mr. Gauld,

Will you accept this expression of my deep regret at the death of your son? His career was so splendid that we might have expected fine results in the future. Such a noble life we think was needed longer on earth; but he filled full the short span he was allotted here; and I believe that he has been promoted to higher service. The sacrifice of our best must mean that some great blessing is being purchased for the world; and I cannot but hold that the kingdom of righteousness is being advanced somehow. With deep sympathy,

I am yours sincerely, Robt A. Falconer

Notes from King George V of England and University of Toronto President Robert A. Falconer, to the family of Lieutenant Gordon Smith Mellis Gauld, following his death in World War I.

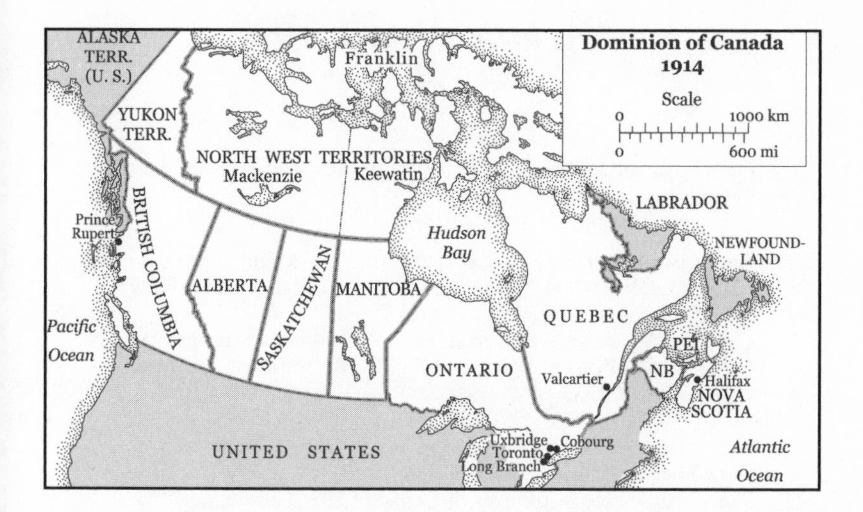

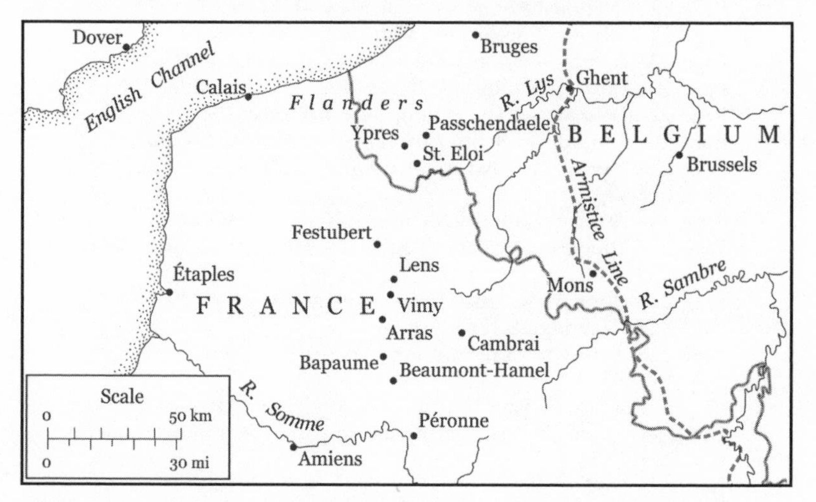

Sites of some of the major battles in France and Belgium fought by Canadian troops.

Acknowledgments

Grateful acknowledgment is made for permission to reprint the following:

Cover portrait: Detail (colourized) from black and white photo, "Miss McLean, 1904," Waldren Studios Collection, Box 54, File 103, Dalhousie University Archives.
Cover background: Detail from photo of Canadian troops marching past Sir Robert Borden, July, 1918, National Archives of Canada PA-002735

Page 218: Courtesy of the author.
Page 219: Uxbridge-Scott Museum.
Page 220: National Archives of Canada C-014135.
Page 221: National Archives of Canada C-036116.
Page 222: National Archives of Canada PA-30282.
Page 223 (upper): National Archives of Canada PA-000568.
Page 223 (lower): National Archives of Canada PA-000832.
Page 224: War Poster Collection, Rare Books and Special Collections Division, McGill University Libraries, Montreal, Canada.
Page 225 (upper): The Art Archive / Imperial War Museum Photo Archive IWM.
Page 225 (lower): National Archives of Canada PA-122515.
Page 226 (upper): Courtesy of Archives, Hospital for Sick Children.
Page 226 (lower): National Archives of Canada PA-022995.
Page 227: Uxbridge-Scott Museum.
Page 228: Courtesy of the author.

Page 229: Maps by Paul Heersink/Paperglyphs. Map data © 2002 Government of Canada with permission from Natural Resources Canada.

The author thanks, first and foremost, her editor, Sandy Bogart Johnston, whose research and inspired editing were of enormous help in shaping Eliza's story. Reference librarians at the Guelph Public Library were always patient and wonderful at answering questions and locating song lyrics. The author's thanks go to Laurel Marsolais, Cathy Taylor, Mary Ramatar and Nancy Clarke. Thanks also to Claire Mackay, who helped with information and moral support.

Thanks to Barbara Hehner for her careful checking of the manuscript; to Allan McGillivray, curator of the Uxbridge-Scott Museum; and to Dr. Desmond Morton, historian and author of such books as *Marching to Armageddon*, for sharing his vast expertise so willingly.

In memory of my uncle
Lieutenant Gordon Smith Mellis Gauld M.C.,
who was killed when his plane
crashed in March, 1918.
He was twenty-five and
he called my mother "Monkeyshines."

And

For my cousin Ailsa Margaret Little,
who remembers Eliza's war
and shares her memories with me.

About the Author

Jean Little grew up hearing tales about her Uncle Gordon. His full name was Gordon Smith Mellis Gauld, the surnames of his four grandparents.

He was the oldest boy in her mother's family and was about to enter law school when a German U-boat sank the civilian passenger ship the *Lusitania*. When he learned of the women and children who had been killed, Gordon Gauld joined the Royal Flying Corps and became an Observer (we would call him a navigator). He also helped train young pilots.

Like Jack and Rufus, Gordon and his best friend fell in love with the same girl. The two young men tossed a coin to decide which of them should propose first. Gordon's friend won the toss, but not the girl. Her telegram accepting Gordon's proposal reached him too late. He died when his plane crashed over England just eight months before the war ended.

His younger brother, Harvey, returned home from the War late at night. Unwilling to rouse his family in the middle of the night, he climbed in through his uncle's dining-room window. His cousin Agnes screamed the house down when she found him, in the morning, asleep on the floor.

After months of searching for Gordon's letters home during World War I, the author found them during the writing of this book — in much the same way that Eliza found her diary after it had been missing for months, tucked away behind some furniture. Jean used elements from Gordon's life, and from other family stories, in writing *Brothers Far from Home*.

Legally blind since birth and now having only light perception, Jean is always accompanied by her guide dog, Pippa. A voracious reader of talking books now that she can no longer read print, Jean loves reading and writing as much as Eliza does. She has been writing since she was twelve — in fact, Belle's short poem near the end of this book is one Jean wrote when she was only ten. And she manages to keep writing with the help of her talking computer, even though her household is much busier than it was a few years ago, now that her great-niece and great-nephew are living with "Auntie" and their grandmother, Jean's sister Pat. Life is further complicated by their eight pets.

Orphan at My Door, Jean Little's first book in the Dear Canada series, won the Canadian Library Association Book of the Year Award in 2002. Jean has written over thirty-five books, including novels, picture books, a book of short stories and poetry, and two autobiographies — *Stars Come Out Within* and *Little by Little.* Books such as *Orphan at My Door* and *Mama's Going to Buy You a Mockingbird, Listen for the Singing, Mine for Keeps, From Anna, His Banner Over Me* and *Hey World, Here I Am!* have won her many prestigious awards, including the Ruth Schwartz Award, the Canada Council Children's Literature Prize, the Violet Downey Award, the Little, Brown Canadian Children's Book Award and the Boston Globe-Horn Book Honor Book Award. She received the Vicky Metcalf Award in 1974 for her Body of Work, and is a member of the Order of Canada. Her newest picture book, with illustrator Werner Zimmermann, is *Pippin the Christmas Pig.*

Jean makes regular visits to schools to meet her many readers. On one trip she mentioned her upcoming book, *Brothers Far from Home.* A student asked her if "regular people" could be heroes too. Jean told the class that she believed all heroes were regular people most of the time. She went on to surprise them by saying that they themselves had probably been heroes *already.* Then she surprised them again by telling them that they had probably already been villains, too.

While the events described and some of the characters in this book may be based on actual historical events and real people, Eliza Bates is a fictional character created by the author, and her diary is a work of fiction.

National Library of Canada Cataloguing in Publication

Little, Jean, 1932-
Dear Canada, brothers far from home : the World War I diary of Eliza Bates / Jean Little.

(Dear Canada)
ISBN 0-439-96900-X

1. World War, 1914-1918–Juvenile fiction. I. Title. II. Series.

PS8523.I77D43 2003 jC813'.54 C2003-901312-X
PZ7

6 5 4 3 2 Printed in Canada 04 05 06 07

The display type was set in Caxton Book Italic.
The text was set in Galliard.

Printed in Canada
First printing June 2003

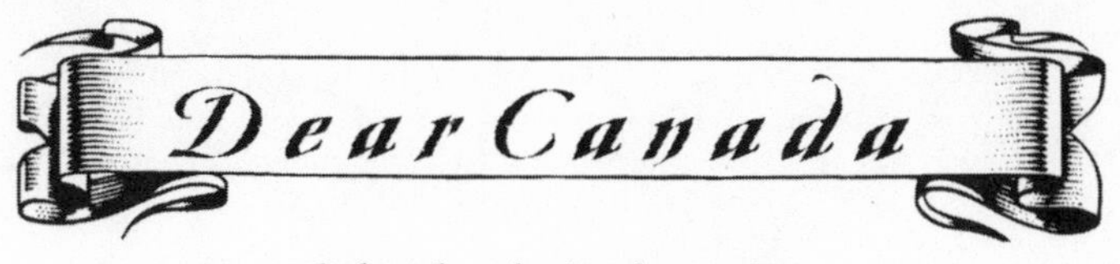

Other books in the series:

A Prairie as Wide as the Sea
The Immigrant Diary of Ivy Weatherall
by Sarah Ellis

Orphan at My Door
The Home Child Diary of Victoria Cope
by Jean Little

With Nothing but Our Courage
The Loyalist Diary of Mary MacDonald
by Karleen Bradford

Footsteps in the Snow
The Red River Diary of Isobel Scott
by Carol Matas

A Ribbon of Shining Steel
The Railway Diary of Kate Cameron
by Julie Lawson

Whispers of War
The War of 1812 Diary of Susanna Merritt
by Kit Pearson

Alone in an Untamed Land
The Filles du Roi *Diary of Hélène St. Onge*
by Maxine Trottier